A WHIRLWIND PROFESSION

A WHIRLWIND PROFESSION

By Catherine Miller

iUniverse, Inc.
New York   Bloomington

A Whirlwind Profession

iUniverse books may be ordered through booksellers or by contacting:

iUniverse
1663 Liberty Drive
Bloomington, IN 47403
www.iuniverse.com
1-800-Authors (1-800-288-4677)

Because of the dynamic nature of the Internet, any Web addresses or links contained in this book may have changed since publication and may no longer be valid. The views expressed in this work are solely those of the author and do not necessarily reflect the views of the publisher, and the publisher hereby disclaims any responsibility for them.

ISBN: 978-1-4401-5105-7 (sc)
ISBN: 978-1-4401-5106-4 (ebk)

Library of Congress Control Number: 2009931027

Printed in the United States of America

iUniverse rev. date: 02/01/2010

To my husband, Jack, for being my travel guide here, there, and everywhere but Alaska.

To my kids, for being included in my life's design.

And to my mother, for giving me the chance to wear the dream.

"If you would not be forgotten as soon as you are gone, either write things worth reading or do things worth writing."

—Benjamin Franklin

"Fashions fade; style is eternal."

—Yves Saint Laurent

"Fashion is not something that exists in dresses only. Fashion is in the sky, in the street—fashion has to do with ideas, the way we live, what is happening."

—Coco Chanel

Contents

Acknowledgments

Flaunting my book as a published author would not feel the same without thanking the many people I have encountered along the way. Some of you helped me because I asked for your help. But most of you just gave me a little guidance and inspiration without even knowing it.

Thank you to *Carolyn Neal* of *iUniverse* for assisting me in the publishing process and for helping me fashion my novel for the runway. Thanks also to *John Potts* of *iUniverse* for talking me into getting started, and *Buddy Dow* from *Author house* for his interesting conversations and coaching about marketing.

Thanks to *Jupiter Images Unlimited* for their front cover design by *Liquid Library* in conjunction with the book cover designers from *iUniverse*.

Special thanks to *Erin Miller*, for her mannequin illustration and for understanding what kind of art concept I was looking for. Thanks also to her teachers from the *TVCSD* for showing her how to dress for success and how to display her artistic talents.

Thank you to *Johnny Miller* for assisting me with technical support on the computer and for not making me nervous by pretending that we lost all of the information.

Thank you to the professors in the Journalism and Communications Department at *C. W. Post Long Island University*, and to my co-writers from way back on the staff of *The Pioneer* for their words of encouragement.

Thank you to my sister, *Patricia Russo*, for sharing with me your love of the English language, ambitions, and clothes!

Thank you to my brothers, *Edwin, Robert, Thomas,* and *William Carlson,* for protecting me from the harmful suitors who tried to put me and my book on the Worst-Dressed List.

Thanks to my niece, *Dorianne,* for letting me borrow your name, career goals, and wild sense of fashion.

Thanks also to my other nieces and nephews, *Christina, Jaclyn, Katie, Joey, Eddie, and Brendan* for filling me in on the current trends of New York college life and for looking very fashionable doing it!

Thank you to *Dianna, Karyn, Julia, Emily, and Natalie, "The Future Fashion Models of New York!"*

Special thanks to *Kelly Miller*, and *Kristen Mingione*, for their beautiful creations in fashion design, which sparked the idea to write this book. Thanks also to *John, Lynne,* and *John* for their rides to school and my kid's inclusions in band practices and videos, which gave me more time to devote to my writing.

Thank you to my husband, *Jack Miller*, for providing the tickets for the shows, concerts, and Broadway plays. Thanks also to the other people from Long Island who enjoyed them with us.

Thank you to the people of *NYC* for lending me the energy and excitement to accurately describe what goes on behind (and in front of) the scenes in the fashion world, music setting, entertainment industry, restaurant business, world of politics, and beyond.

Thank you to *the Nokia Theatre, Hilton Hotel, Marriot Marquis, New Yorker Hotel, Tavern On the Green, Metropolitan Museum of Art, St. Patrick's Cathedral, Café d'Alsace, La Grenouille Restaurant, DJ Reynolds Irish Pub, Niko's Mediterranean Grill, Trattoria Dopo Teatro, The Museum of Modern Art, The Empire State Building, Radio City Music Hall, The Fashion Institute of Technology, Gracie Mansion, ESPN Zone, Bloomingdales, Macy's, Ripley's NY, Starbucks, The New York Public Library, The Hayden Planetarium, Rockefeller Center, United Nations Hall, JC Penney, Madison Square Garden, Barnes and Noble Booksellers, Wolman's Ice Rink, and Planet Hollywood,* for just being in NYC.

Special thanks to *Vanity Fair* and *Condé Nast Publications, Victoria's Secret, Fuse, YouTube, Entertainment Weekly, The New York Times,* and *Gentlemen's Quarterly* for accessorizing my work of fiction.

Thank you to the *Hollywood Foreign Press Association* and *organizers of the award show,* for being such good sports about me fictitiously bringing the *Golden Globes* to NYC.

Thank you to my mother, *Patricia Carlson,* for being my role model.

Thank you to *Noreen, Doreen, Susan*, and *Maria Carlson* for being in the same boat when it comes to dressing in America.

Thanks also to the *Russos, Millers, Cooks*, and *Knepps*, for the good memories that I wouldn't trade for anything.

Belated thanks to *Christina Fox,* for getting me into the movies at a very young age; *Thomas Fox,* for his great sense of humor and musical talent; and to *Catherine Carlson*, for showing me how to save my words for a sunny day.

Thank you to my father, *Edwin Carlson*, who never got the chance to read my book, but who is still laughing up in heaven about getting me through my interviewing class.

Thank you to *Elvis Costello, Journey, Frank Sinatra, Twisted Sister, Coldplay, and Green Day* for the use of brief quotations of lyrics from their real songs (and one fake one) embodied in this contemporary work of fiction.

Thank you to the *US Virgin Islands* for the use of their dream destination in this book about NYC and to those happy campers in the *Florida Keys* for their novel personalities.

Thank you to my friends at *LifeTouch Photo Studio* for understanding why I had to quit after receiving my Certificate of Achievement in photography, and to *The Feds* for helping me to earn the money for publication fees.

Finally, thank you to *Larry Dale, Kathi Wittkamper,* and the *entire editorial department* of *iUniverse* for your professional editing services that made this book presentable to a world of stylish readers.

Because I have a fondness for fashionable people and cities all over the USA(and in other countries in our universe), I wear the colors of red, white, and blue proudly and most often. But, since I've lived here my whole life, my personal campaign ribbon says *I Love New York*. Therefore, I would like to say thank you to the Brookhaven politicians for the Setauket—Port Jeff Station Greenway Trail. Readers who want to help preserve the wide open spaces on Long Island can send their tax-deductible contributions to:

Friends of the Greenway
c/o The Village Trust
P.O. Box 2596
Setauket, NY 11733
or log on to:
www.threevillagecommunitytrust.org

Chapter 1

The Winter Gala

"All of this red is appalling," I whispered to Mary at the fabulous Winter Gala, anxiously waiting for one of my sapphire or greenish hues to appear on the runway. For me, red is always a florid shade that makes my complexion look ashen and pale. Most of this fashion world, however, seems to think it is a vibrant magnet that attracts attention to anyone looking to call attention to themselves—especially Mary, a blonde with dark eyebrows, who is always applying some kind of ruby lipstick to her lips to match what she is wearing. I have to admit it looks good on her. She was the one who insisted that I keep it in my line, if not for any other reason than that she is my biggest fan. She also happens to be my best friend and my number one client. I had to include it just for her.

"Even though I know the design is of primary importance here, some articles of clothing simply look better in certain colors," Mary said. "So much for being unique," I said jokingly, as another boring strapless gown made its formal entrance into society. My comments flowed easily during a major lull in the yearly fashion show. I always try to pass the time along with mindless chatter until my big moment arrives so I don't get too nervous. "There are so many dumb-looking party dresses mixed in." Mary made an absurd face. "Where in the world would you wear that?" she asked. "Maybe to a Republican convention!" I answered, and we both started to laugh.

"Here it is!" I stood up, applauded, and waved, which is customary for a designer to do when a model comes out on the catwalk displaying something from her label. The strip of infamous guy celebrities sitting right behind me were watching intently, so I smiled and nodded and made the gestures very quickly. The *Tina Fashion* I chose was a sea-green mohair sweater-dress just above the knee, with a big, wide pearl belt that clipped to the side at the waist. Brenda, the model, wore lacy stockings and big T-strap baby-doll shoes in aqua with a silver buckle on each side, which accessorized nicely.

"What a relief," I said. "It all came together. Now if that baby sells, we could be in for a mean Christmas season." Mary agreed with me. "Brenda doesn't have too far to go before she's in the big leagues. Her right-then-left crossover walk showed poise and confidence, which is exactly what your creation needed—a flair for the dramatic. Your design outshined them all, and Brenda definitely has potential."

I secretly wanted her to be chosen to model my *Tina Fashion* because she has long legs and an arrogance about her. In my opinion, she was already beyond being America's-top-model material. She has literally already secured a place for herself in the extreme high-fashion world. My tags need an edge, and my old rhythm styles need someone like Brenda to attract a target audience. "Beauty and sophistication with an attitude. That's exactly what she radiates during a show. Thank God, it was a success!"

We hurried into the after-show party, through the white marble entranceway into another magnificent room in the New York Public Library, because in this business you can't diss the organizers. My winter-white wool suit was starting to get uncomfortable, and my silver-city-pink lipstick was wearing off. "What I'd give to be in a pair of faded blue jeans right now," I whispered under my breath.

"Michael, how have you been?" It was my neighbor from a number of years ago, standing in the corner holding a champagne glass in one hand and a bouquet of pink roses in the other. He had been leaning against a white raised sculpture of a face that resembled Hercules, or Galileo, coming out of the wall. "For you, sweetheart," he whispered, as he kissed me on the cheek and handed me the flowers. I held them up to my nose to feel the soft velvety petals and capture the sweet fragrance. "Umm … pink roses are my favorite. Michael, you're the best."

"I'm in town doing some public relations work for the production company that happens to be sponsoring this fashion show for the library. You're going to make a million with your design this time, Tina. Everyone is raving about it. Let's tour New York City tomorrow. Nothing will satisfy my hunger except that new burger place on Fifth Avenue. I have so many engaging topics to discuss with you. We've been detached for too long."

I knew he was right. I missed our rendezvous in the city, and I have always had a thing for him. He lived in the apartment across the hall for two straight years, and we were just getting close when our careers jolted us apart. "You look fantastic," I told him. "Let's just say in shape," he quipped. "Of course I'll go. Give me a call in the morning," I said.

By this time, I knew Mary was impressed because she was giving me surreptitious glances sideways. I waved my hand as a signal for her to keep her mouth shut, and I was so happy that she played it cool until we were far away from the building. The white lights lining the cement steps in front of the library and the Christmas wreaths on the two lion statues of *Patience* and *Fortitude* looked so beautiful at night.

"Let's summarize," said Mary in a tantalizing voice that sounded completely unafraid of losing me as a friend after all of these years. "It seems that tonight was your lucky night. I bet you're glad we followed our simple plan this time. It was fate that you ran into Michael. You guys were like two luminescent stars colliding in the atmosphere—just like in the Spiral Galaxy at the Hayden Planetarium. He was an affectionate neighbor, wasn't he?"

She could tell what I was thinking by the mysterious smile that I was wearing. The past is unalterable, and the future is looking marvelous. I didn't want to jinx myself by saying too much, since I was trying to keep my career my first priority. "It would be nice to get involved in a relationship with Michael, but I hope it's not a poor time to shake up the Earth," I said.

We summoned a taxi because our feet were starting to hurt from all of the walking we were doing in our high heels. Besides, the chill in the air was turning our breath into smoky circles, and I didn't want to catch the flu with my upcoming busy schedule. As we drove away, the lights on the tall blue spruce Christmas tree at Rockefeller Plaza became a radiant blur. "The sequoias out in California are beautiful too, Mary, but this is the coolest tree that NYC has ever had so far. It's giving the wool-coat-clad New Yorkers, and the tourists, a good feeling while they are standing above the ice rink listening to the seasonal Christmas music."

She took a crisp new hundred-dollar bill, with the face of Ben Franklin, out of her wallet and waved it in front of the driver's nose. "I have the cab fare this time," she told me as we approached her apartment building with the green canopy over the entrance and the brass-buttoned doorman guarding the door. I remember we used to sit in front of the window and critique what the people on the street below us were wearing. Her luxury apartment was high enough for a clear view and there weren't any guard rails blocking the double-pane glass window, even though that was against the building code laws. Sometimes we'd climb up the stairs to the flat, tarred roof to try and catch a tan. There weren't that many sunny spots on this side of the city, and Mary was a sun worshiper if I ever knew one.

"Oh, by the way," she said, before she was ready to get out. "Getting back to the topic of the color red— scientifically, I think it is considered a hot color because of something that has to do with our human body state. We are filled with blood and are therefore considered warm-blooded animals. When the blood is in our veins, it's as blue as the color of my lips when I'm very cold. They're probably blue right now. Anyway, as a secretary, I'm not very good at biology. All I know is that your nose turns the same color as a Macintosh apple when you have a sip of alcohol. Red is a hot color to me in fashion. But, Tina, your design was absolutely stunning in sea green."

As she got out of the cab, she turned around and said, "Way to make your dreams come true." Her genuine sincerity did not catch me by surprise, because she is always so good at wearing BS. "Thanks for being there for me, Mary. That's what I like about you. You're very pretentious, and you never know what the hell you're talking about!" I shouted back. The disheveled taxi driver thought he was funny by asking me trivia questions the entire twenty-minute ride to my studio apartment. So I played along, happy that his simulated game show was taking my mind off the evening's excitement.

As soon I unlocked the door, I slipped into my satin nightgown and a warm velour sweatshirt, and then I placed my yellow ceramic kettle on the smooth burner for a nice steaming cup of hot tea. I pressed the button to retrieve the messages on my answering machine, and the lyrical voices of my closest critics contributed to my good mood. "Bravo, Tina, a job well done," from Daniel, my friend from graphic design. Beep. "Your stylish fashion exceeded our expectations," from the New York Public Library. Beep. And the next one, of course, from my sister Lauren. "Tina, I apologize for not being there tonight, but news travels like bottle rockets in NYC, and there's already a whole group of designers waiting to form an alliance with you. Way to go!" she said. Beep.

"This faithful answering machine is so great to have relayed all of those welcome messages to me," I said to myself. "It doesn't give off any radio frequency emissions either, like the cell phones nowadays. I'll have to keep it as long as possible and replay those sentiments over and over like a classic song on the radio."

I headed into my studio to finish shading in one of my sketches with a smile on my face, fully aware that this was the start of something big. From my circle top window, I could see the lights of the city. It was the exact view that lured me to this vicarious fashion center of the world. I was feeling thankful that I will never suffer from ennui in this career in a beautiful place like this, and I slept like a baby.

Chapter 2

The Lunch Date

The hustle and bustle caused by a city full of humans under my window has always taken the place of an alarm clock for me. When the daily action begins here, it shakes me like the rugged arm of someone in my bed shouting, "Wake up! Wake up!" The turbulent force of all of those people outside hastily tending to unfinished business always makes me feel like I will be missing something if I don't get up right away. The first thing I did this morning, before my beauty routine, is zip up my sweatshirt and look outside to check out the view.

Michael and I planned to start out way before noon, pretending it was a Saturday, so we'd feel healthy and energetic enough for a whirlwind tour of NYC. The weather was sunny and beautiful, and I knew we'd be doing a lot of walking, talking, shopping, and unearthing. I felt like being impulsive. I was absolutely starving, and I really couldn't wait to have a well-done burger and an ice-cold Coke Zero with my old confidant.

He was looking cool and casual when he picked me up, sporting a four o'clock shadow already this early in the day. That is exactly what taking the day off is all about. I figured that he would be unshaven and wearing a pair of faded blue jeans and a thermal sweatshirt, since he also liked to take a break from the *Gentlemen's Quarterly*-style business suits required daily in his own demanding profession. I remember that's what I liked about him. He has a dressed-up look and a relaxed look. Neither one of us was into going to a fancy restaurant after handling the affairs and program of events the previous night.

"*Wow*, Tina," he said as he looked up at the board at the burger joint. "It's a virtually unknown place. They really only have around three things on the menu here." We sat at a table right behind the neon sign and an old theatre curtain pulled closed. It was kind of out of the way, but just far enough from the noise of the city to make it a good place to catch up on recent happenings.

"Don't get the fries with the cheese sauce. They will make you feel nauseous all day," I advised him. "I think I'm going to get the second thing on the board—the All American. It's all about tradition when you're ordering a burger."

I put my napkin across my lap so I wouldn't spill anything on my favorite jeans and thought about what Michael just said. "That inherited way of ordering a burger is great if you can dress it up a bit," I replied. "But too much cultural continuity in anything can be a drag. One thing's for sure. The cheese sauce on those fries gives me the same feeling as the paisley pattern on that guy's shirt."

We made it an extra-easy order for the waitress, as if her job was not easy enough with such a limited menu. She was wearing a white apron over a pair of skinny jeans and a pair of slip-on sneakers. My guess was that she was probably a lot older than she looked. "Even when there's sauce already on it, I pour a bottle of ketchup on my hamburger anyway. I was never deprived of dressing when I was young. That's probably why I ended up with a career in fashion designing," I told Michael.

The waitress did not waste any time placing our order, and Michael grabbed a sour dill pickle spear and tasted a few salty french fries before beginning the conversation. "Putting the insignificant matters of my public relations firm aside, because my business matters have been excellent, to say the least, I'd like to say that I've missed you so much in the past few years. And after observing you in action last night, and I hope I'm not being rude here, you seem to be one of the few—in the high-class fashion designer category from midtown—who hasn't sold out. Do you agree, Tina?" he asked.

"Well thanks, Michael. I think I understand what the heck you just said, and I'll just take that as a compliment," I answered. After erasing my puzzled look, I thought about it for a minute and decided to zap him back with my intelligence. "Everyone is either out to make money or into performing acts of charity, and sometimes you don't know if they're in the business with some ulterior motive. It can be a little disconcerting. The longer you deal with the different prospects, the sharper you become at spying the ones who are in it to ruin the fashion world. Personally, I work to achieve a flamboyant flair with my designs as I pursue an ambitious career—not to incite shock value or to be labeled a goody two-shoes."

"I'm glad to see you're as wide awake as ever with your own observations," he said, pouring the rest of his beverage into the lemon-flavored ice. "And you prate endlessly, just like you used to." He flashed his famous toothy smile, showing all of his pearly whites, and winked. "We sound like such pseudo intellectuals, don't we?" he asked. We both laughed as the waitress placed another bottle of ketchup on the table in front of me.

I could feel my true feelings for him starting to return. I wasn't one to let down my guard that easily, and this feeling of vulnerability made me a little insecure. I loved the fact that he tried to analyze me, and I knew that he was just trying to justify his decision to move away for the sake of his career. He is the only person in the world who makes me feel individually designed when I see him, and the only guy in the world who knows how to lighten things up.

"Enough talk about work. What's new in your personal life?" I asked eagerly. Surprised at the question, his dark brown eyes quickly glanced away. "Well, I've had some insignificant relationships with a few women, parting ways with nominal hurt feelings. How about you?" Michael asked me. I tried to wheedle my way out of answering that question too, but he was persistent. "How about you?" he asked me again. "Okay, let's just say the numerous men I've encountered in the fashion world have either been noncommittal, too into themselves, or gay." Michael just shook his head and laughed again, but I think I might have said something to perk his interest.

When the check came, he grabbed it from my hands with a firm swiftness and said, "I'll get that, babe." I really liked the fact that he fought me for the check. Then we headed out onto Fifth Avenue, into the bright sunshine, and when he held my hand to cross the street, he never let it go.

We walked around NYC the entire day—people watching and culture shopping. We toured the Museum of Modern Art and studied all kinds of naked statues and controversial artwork. We stopped in at almost every single bookstore on every single block, read signs reviewing the plays on Broadway, and sampled a lot of new music. Michael discovered the tribute to one of the most famous Beatles quite by accident. It was in the form of a stone circle right under his feet. He had forgotten it was right here in Strawberry Fields, Central Park West.

"Imagine if he was really buried here," I said. "You know that he used to live in that apartment building across the street. I can still picture him walking around in his striped poncho and round wire-framed glasses."

We went up and down on the elevators in Bloomingdale's, marveling at the beautiful but very expensive clothing on the racks. As I slid each hanger to the right, I carefully studied each article and estimated the amount of time and work that went into creating each one. "I was introduced to one of the buyers the other day," I told Michael. "She told me that they are very, very selective with their designs. She is extremely interested in one of mine. It's an electric blue halter top with silver beading. I have Mary trying to clinch a deal with them at this very moment."

I pointed out some mannequins in the window of a bridal salon that was one of the first to include my fashion in their seasonal show when I was merely a novice at designing. It was a bridal gown with a white satin hood and imitation fur, with matching satin gauntlets all the way up the arms, almost to the elbow. I was always telling Mary that if I ever got married, that's the look I would go for. Mike wasn't sure whether or not he liked the accompanying tuxedo jacket on the male mannequin. "A guy who would wear that would be an avarice bridegroom, to say the least. I would predict that the bride herself would be paying for the wedding," he joked.

"Don't mind my nasty comments, Tina," he added. "That's okay, Michael. That kind of sarcasm can't really get you into trouble now. You're not that young anymore. You're older and wiser and established in your own right," I replied. But I knew I didn't really have to talk sense into him about tactfulness or finances, since he is in the business of public relations.

Mike met a few friends on the street in front of the library, and he shook hands with them and proceeded to introduce me. "Chris and Joe, I'd like you to meet Tina," he said. I had actually met both guys already at a *Vanity Fair* magazine cover photo shoot. I was there because I designed the outfit that the model was wearing, and Chris was there doing the lighting for his friend Joe, the photographer. At times, meeting familiar faces on the streets of New York City can be tricky. You can't always match them with their names, suits, or business cards. "I suppose you don't remember me," I said. "Are you kidding?" he replied. "A black silk jumpsuit, silver hoop earrings, and three inch stilettos. An extraordinary *Tina Design*, which worked wonders for the cover of *Vanity Fair*. I was only there to help with the lighting, but it was sensational," he said. "How come you didn't go to the after-party?"

"Wouldn't you know that it was the very same day that the burglar alarm went off in my studio?" I answered.

"And I rarely miss an after-party. It's so important to mingle in my profession."

"Well, maybe you'll be at the next one. It was such a success that I know they'll invite you back," he said. "If I recall, you were also wearing black—a scoop-neck ribbed sweater-dress that just might have matched your eye makeup."

"How nice of you to have noticed," was all I could come up with. In my mind, I was questioning whether or not someone in this small group put him up to saying that. Anyway, I took the compliment and ran with it, and the fact that Chris remembered how I was dressed seemed to impress Michael, I could tell. He just stood there staring and grinning at the two of us, like he was amazed at the conversation that just took place.

When a freelance dance troupe started a routine right below the concrete steps of the library, we watched them for a while and delayed our stroll down the block. The group of eight *Thriller Zombies* were really very good on their feet, so Michael threw a ten-dollar bill into the open hard suitcase that they had set up on the sidewalk. They were dressed in rags, and they had dark black eyes sunken into painted white faces. The last time they danced here, they looked just like the King of Pop in fedoras and leather pants.

A few minutes later, I found a metro card in the street by a blue-painted bus stop, so I bent down to pick it up. "I wonder if there's any money left on it," I said to

Michael. "Carry it with you, Tina, and the next time we take the subway you can try to swipe it. It will be just like trying your luck by playing lotto. Just don't do it during rush hour. You'll anger some commuter who's in a hurry to get home."

"The woman wearing the tan skirt suit and red beret at the information booth will tell me if there's a zero balance," I said. "It might be safer than causing some guy in a dark raincoat from Long Island to miss his train and home-cooked meal."

When the sun started to go behind the tall buildings, we ducked into a Starbucks for a late afternoon coffee and a foamy hot café latte, and it was cozy and warm and exactly the boost of caffeine we needed for the long walk home. "The barista sprayed whipped cream on her green apron as she was topping your latte," I said to Michael. "She was very upset. Did you see her do it?"

"Yes. It was kind of funny. She must be new there," Michael replied. "She'll probably have to attend another barista training course to learn how not to do that," I added. The conversation flowed, the weather held up, and I could tell that the chemistry was there between us, even though neither one of us said it out loud.

Chapter 3

The Concert

We had great seats for the concert at the Nokia Theatre, and it was really passionate fun to see my sketches showing off on stage. It had been a slightly different kind of challenge trying to design the band's clothing for this tour, which had stops on it that were a step up from venues like the very popular Knitting Factory—at least from a fashion designer's perspective. Today's musicians often ask fashion designers to assist them, and this group happened to be related to longtime friends of ours who really know how to dress. They pride themselves on their sophisticated image and esoteric skill. Dramatic alternative bands are much more common now, and this group will probably be one of the lucky few to keep their place in the limelight. The young rock 'n' roll society likes bands that portray mystery and glamour along with giving the world good music. By seeing the crowd's reaction tonight, they seemed to measure up to the fans' expectations. They changed their clothes four times in the two-and-a-half hour timeframe of the concert. They were charming to look at and a fresh sound to the ears when they toned it down a bit.

My *Tina Fashions* were only for the main ticket, not for the virtually unknown warm-up band that did quite nicely on their own, although not really with their clothing. They displayed a bad boy persona by wearing rude messages on their black T-shirts and colorful tattooed artwork on their bodies. I knew that they had potential in the music world because of their well-written, incisive lyrics, and strong, deep voices; but then again, I'm a fashion designer, not a talent scout. Mary was totally into the bass player, who seemed to be staring directly at her, not the hundreds of screaming young females who each paid thirty dollars a ticket to get in. In gratitude for her boy toy, she held up her cell phone and requested an encore, and the whole situation was amusing, to say the least. "Mary, you've got at least twenty years on him," I shouted. She just laughed and said, "Age doesn't matter. Didn't you learn that yet?" It was so easy for Mary to fit in with a younger crowd. I, on the other hand, was having a slightly harder time focusing on the whole scene.

"Designing the sleeves that the guitar player requested

gave me a little trouble this time. She didn't want them to get in the way while she was playing. I fashioned the wide bell sleeves mainly for the singer with the microphone, not the ones playing the instruments," I explained. "Luckily, I only have to design these clothes, and not really sew them," I added. "Whether you're tailoring or designing clothes for the band, their playing can be affected if things are not right."

"Good musicians worry about the musical aspect first and image second," Lauren piped in. "Well they should anyway. Unless they're just 'selling out.'"

"To be a music idol in America you have to have the right clothes and the right music. A musician does not want to stop in the middle of a song to pull a sleeve out of an instrument. A break like that could ruin the tune, cause a tear, or reveal a singer lip-synching. Most good guitar players know that it's easier to play when you keep your fingernails short. They also know that no matter how fashionable you want to look while playing, shorter sleeve lengths are much more practical. It's common-sense dressing, in a way. It's why ice skaters never wear material dragging on the ice, and dancers' gowns are tailored to the perfect length—just hitting the floor—so they don't trip," I explained. Mary did not hear a thing I said. She was totally mesmerized by the guy in the band.

After the warm-up, it was too loud for us to carry on any more conversation. We happened to be sitting by the compact speakers, which made it even worse.

My ears were ringing, and I realized that I could take the concert experience a lot better in my younger days, even though the music was as great on the radio as ever. The combination of lights and special effects gets to you after a while, when you've had too much radio frequency aimed at your head. It's sort of like wearing an itchy wool hat.

They were filming a music video for *Fuse*, and the cameraman tried to capture us a few times, no doubt to give me the credit for the designs. When the spotlight was on us, I pasted a smile on my face and swayed back and forth to the songs anyway, waving my arms over my head just like we used to, pretending to have a good time. "Our thanks to *Tina the Fashion Designer* for our wardrobe!" the lead singer shouted. So I stood up excitedly and took a bow, completely oblivious to the drug addict behind me throwing fuzz balls on my shoulder.

At intermission, I left Mary and Lauren in their seats to go backstage and socialize for a few minutes. The band introduced me to their amazing technicians and very smart production manager. "Great first set," I commented. "You carried the designs off well. Everyone looks wonderful." Some sarcastic stagehand, who was busy plugging in an amplifier, mumbled under his breath, "You have a great set, too." But I just ignored him. I didn't realize until later that the zipper on my mock turtleneck sweater had slipped down a little too low with the help of some guy's magnetic wand.

I didn't want to overstay my welcome because they were obviously busy back there. So I disappeared into the eclectic and much younger crowd and made my way to the refreshment stand for three bottles of water and a blue concert T-shirt. The "merch" guy held up an adult medium so everyone could see it. It was twice the price, and a size smaller than the black concert T-shirts of yesterday, but it was somehow vintage anyway. It didn't have a long list of venue stops on the tour written down the back—just the name of the band penned in white script across a burst of colorful fireworks: A Whirlwind Profession.

When the lavender spotlights went down again, the singer came out in my fabulously designed indigo wrap minidress accented by silver drop earrings, and the crowd went wild. I could tell they were having a blast, and it made me feel really good to be part of the whole scene.

After the concert, Mary insisted on picking up some fast food from the little Chinese restaurant across the street because she was famished. Everyone else in NYC seemed to have switched to sushi, but Mary still liked this old Asian place. By the time we came back out, her face was glowing from a bad reaction to the super dark, orange sweet and sour sauce. It was clashing with her dress. What a funny feeling of history repeating itself. Bright pink did not look good with the shade of Mary's new complexion. "We should petition the governor to call in the Board of Health for the permanent removal of MSG," she said.

"Are you okay, Mary?" I asked. "I'll just take my dress off when I get home," she replied. "But that could turn out just as dangerous. I was having such a good night, too. It just proves you really shouldn't try to go back in time. You should never go back."

As we made our way to the parking garage, the wind picked up, and I quickly put on my wool crocheted hat and matching scarf. Then I covered my entire head with the hood of my gray wool coat. We could have taken a taxi home, but we decided to pile into Lauren's yellow sports car instead. The lights of the Empire State Building were bouncing off of her rearview mirror like a pink pastel crayon reflecting off of a piece of foil. There was a new billboard in Times Square that I had never seen before advertising the band. It had hologram images of the musicians we just saw in concert constantly changing on a diamond vision screen, and they were all wearing the fashions that I designed—skin-tight wrap dresses in indigo, yellow, and green with straps and cut outs everywhere. "Beautiful and impressive promotional work," Lauren said, as she swerved to avoid an oncoming car.

Her comment about the new advertisement made me start thinking about Michael and his PR work again. I was wondering what he's been up to. Almost a week had gone by since our lunch date, and I was hoping to see him some night of this weekend again. He's usually the first one to fill me in on new technological advances like this one in the city, especially if my work is involved.

Lauren turned into a race car driver when she was behind the wheel, so we made it home in what seemed to be no time at all. She just kept weaving in and out of traffic, like thread being pulled out of a seam in a NYC skyline. "I have to make it home by midnight, or Jimmy will wig out," she said.

Mary was familiar with Lauren's husband, and she knew that I thought he was an arrogant boss—which was the least bad way, on my list of bad ways, to describe him. Neither one of us knew what to say. Of course, we wouldn't want her to get in trouble. I could never really understand why she chose marriage to him over life as the ultimate bachelorette anyway. She could be dating all the fun guys here in NYC. I figured out early on that it must have been his sharp Italian nose and dark eyes that attracted her to him. Jimmy's the type of guy who wears a black leather jacket with a constant bank roll of money in his side pocket. Mary, however, has always preferred the beach-blonde type of guy wearing a Hawaiian shirt and khaki shorts. She's the one always waving the money in a relationship. I just looked at both of them like they were crazy, and we let the moment pass.

In my mind I tried to put everything in my sister's surroundings in perspective. Lauren lives a very good life. It is true that it was not always easy for her to raise her kids up until now with such a strong-willed husband. But most of the time she seems happy. She has been trying so hard to make everything work and to have a functional family. She doesn't even have to go out and earn a paycheck if she doesn't want to. Jimmy makes more money in one day running the parking garage than some people make in a month. And they possess a whole corner of the Monopoly board game with their unlimited free parking midtown.

Lauren took a hairpin turn around the corner too fast, and my cell phone and the rest of the contents of my bag fell out all over the back seat. "Better late than never," I said to her, reminding her to slow down. I was referring to her interest in high fashion as well as her driving.

When she dropped me off, I ran upstairs to check my voicemail. "I would just like to confirm a Saturday night dinner date," said the smooth voice on the other end. It was Michael. "If you're into it, I'll pick you up at eight. We'll be double-dating with another couple, so dress fancy, be prepared for small talk, and I'll fill you in when I see you. I'll take a no reply as a yes. See you then, Tina." Beep.

Oh, so sure of himself, I thought. But that was exactly the message that I was hoping for. I went into my studio for awhile to sketch and unwind, and I thought about what I was going to wear this weekend. It's always strange to be on the other side of the drawing board, so to speak: a professional designer having to choose something to wear myself.

Chapter 4

The Double Date

Before I knew it, Michael was standing in the doorway. He looked like a giant silhouette in front of a backdrop of iridescent elevator lights. His gray pinstripe suit complimented his stark white shirt and even darker gray vest. The abstract design on his royal blue, maroon, and silver tie looked like a jagged-edged outline of the tall buildings uptown.

"What a coincidence; we match," I said. "We couldn't have planned a better color combination." I had chosen a shimmery, silver lame' off-the-shoulder cocktail dress that came right to the knees, and a pair of medium heel pumps. "At the risk of sounding full of myself, you look as good as I do," he joked.

We headed downstairs and got into his black Lexus, which was illegally double-parked with hazard lights flashing, and zoomed toward the restaurant. "That was a risky move, Michael," I said. "The last time someone double-parked in front of my studio, they were zapped with a high-priced dry-cleaning ticket. She was a client of mine who stopped in to pick up a design. As she was getting back in her SUV, a fast car drove through a puddle and splashed water up onto the dress. I felt really bad about it. She had to wear a pantsuit that night. "

I pointed to a nearby brick building with a deep ramp. "There's usually room in that parking garage on a Saturday night. Just park in there across the street next time. I know I should have reminded you about that earlier. It's been a while since you've been in the neighborhood. You and my sister's husband are among the elite few who own their own vehicles around here. The only reason Jimmy has a car is because he owns the parking garage downtown. It's right across the street from the Fashion Institute of Technology."

"Let me fill you in on tonight, Tina," Michael said. "We're meeting a dynamic couple, Dori and Rob, at the *Café d' Alsace* French restaurant midtown. He works at the production company, and I believe she's a CEO for a work-from-home computer-based Web site. They've only been dating for about seven months, and it seems that they are hitting it off royally. I don't want to get too personal with the small talk; I just want to reel him in as my right-hand man. They're so hard to find nowadays."

"Relax," I answered. "I can keep the conversation as light as you want." Then I asked pensively, "Is his date into fashion?" Michael said, "Oh yes, big time. You'll see."

We had to worry about where to park again, but in the distance there was a convenient yet expensive parking garage. The weather was iffy, and I hoped that we wouldn't get all windblown walking to the restaurant. Michael handed the attendant the keys reluctantly. He doesn't like to trust anyone with his Lexus. "I've got a spare pair," he said. "Don't dare take it for a spin."

The attendant didn't really know what to make of him. He just glared at him with dark eyes that looked like studs. To tell you the truth, his beady glance made us both a little nervous. I wondered where I've seen him before. It dawned on me that he might be a friend of Lauren's husband. They probably attend parking garage seminars together or something. Michael bundled his coat up and pulled his wool scarf around his neck and didn't say anything else to him. "Keep your fingers crossed, Tina, that my leather gloves are still in it when we come out, or else."

"Oh. That's the spare pair you were referring to," I replied. "I thought for sure you meant the hubcaps."

Dori and Rob were at the coat check counter in the lobby when we arrived. I kept my black velvet jacket with me to wear over my shoulders in case there was a draft at the table, but Dori had Rob check her full-length fur coat. It looked like raccoon fur of some sort. She didn't have to know this, but living in NYC, I was among the group who always despised coats made out of animal fur. She was pushing her luck by wearing one, especially on this side of town.

Her dress underneath was as simple and impressive as the winning fifteen hundred word essay on the topic of "Reality in America" featured in *Vanity Fair* magazine. She could have won a trip to Italy and a *Mont Blanc* pen, for God's sake. It was brown snakeskin with a turtleneck and a big, wide, brown, alligator-leather belt. She was obviously fond of wearing dead animals. I had vowed to myself a long time ago that the *Tina Fashion* insignia would never be used for any garments that were made from the real fur or skins of animals. My tags have a tiny segment written in fine print concerning that matter. Mary wanted me to introduce the cheetah and leopard prints to the line, and I told her "absolutely not!" The zebra print and the color red were enough of a compromise, and much easier to camouflage.

Anyway, Rob and Michael ordered a bottle of White Star, and I let the waitress pour me a glass, which I later sneakily passed on to Michael. He knows I like to drink water or sparkling apple cider when everyone else is drinking champagne. A carbonated and refreshing non-alcoholic boost of vitamin C does wonders for a tired complexion.

I ordered the Gold Coast shrimp, which was stuffed and lying over a bed of rice like a pearl-neck sweater. Michael ordered the filet mignon—medium rare with rosette potatoes that looked like decorative fasteners in the center of a push-up bra. The entrees were high in price, but it was nice to be at a time in our lives when money is no object. There really wasn't anything on the menu less than twenty-nine dollars a plate. This particular restaurant is known for its pocket pastries and croissants.

Rob and Dori both ordered the stuffed quail, which I could barely look at when the waitress brought them to the table. They were little birds with cherry tomatoes propped in their mouths on the plate. It seemed these two were going out of their way to evoke a reaction from me on the subject of dead animals. But I remembered what Michael had said on the way in about keeping the conversation light, and I didn't fall for it. Besides, I found Rob charming, in a way. He seemed to be a blond and blue-eyed version of Michael, but with a slightly more slangy vocabulary, not as good a sense of humor, and an equally impeccable taste in clothing. The whole tab came to three hundred and fifty dollars including the tip, and Michael sprang for the entire evening. We lingered over dessert and shared a few good laughs.

Believe it or not, our pleasant conversation included chats about the possibility of a woman being voted in as vice president, who does the best impressions on *SNL*, which late-night talk show host we all watch, if any, and whether or not we should promote solar heating and energy-saving windmills. "It is unanimous that you-know-who remains the king of late-night TV," said Rob. "When we can all stay awake past ten with our heavy work schedules," Michael said. "The other guy seems to appeal to the twenty-something generation. But, he can be amusing too at times."

"I once read a magazine article in *Entertainment Weekly* on the funny things he did during the writers' strike," I added. "It was a diary, in a sense, and it was hysterical. He said something like he had to keep going to the fridge for some more pomegranate tea—so that he could write down his action to fill up time because no one else was writing any material for him. In the fashion business, we really don't have to worry about strikes too often. The garment workers have a very good union now. But, during that one strike, when we were headed toward the recession, I added to my fashion journal all of the things I will do in my whirlwind profession as a fashion designer in the future. When everyone has money again, I plan to have more than a fun-filled field day with the fashion design world. You can all read it some time. As far as keeping pomegranate iced tea in the refrigerator, fashion designers prefer orange juice or water." Everyone laughed, and we headed toward the parking garage. Dori told Michael that I should display my fashion journal in e-zine form on the computer because the younger generations love to read personal accounts about people dressing up on the Web.

Rob helped Dori put on her raccoon fur while I slipped my arms into the sleeves of my short jacket, and we waited for the car attendants to retrieve our vehicles. I had an uneasy feeling over the fact that she was wearing animal fur on this side of town. As soon as we hit the cold air, as Dori fumbled for a cigarette, a small group holding buckets of red paint ran up the street. They proceeded to splatter the paint on Dori's raccoon fur coat. It was obvious that they were animal rights activists, because they were chanting things like "No animal fur on this side of town!" and "Freedom for animals—no wearing fur!"

Dori didn't cry or anything. In fact, she took it like a good sport. But the coat was ruined, and the look on Michael's face was one of sheer horror. Before anyone could come to Dori's defense, they ran away and disappeared behind one of the brick buildings. "I knew it was going to happen," I whispered to Michael. Dori quickly composed herself and said, "Don't worry, guys. I will not let it ruin a great evening." And Michael added, "Rob, you have quite a catch there. Don't let her go."

Rob helped Dori off with her coat so it wouldn't wreck the interior upholstery of his car, and they sped away shouting thanks to Michael and waving to me. "Nice meeting you," she said, as Rob drove straight through the first red light. But I knew inside, Dori was probably crying.

When we climbed into the Lexus, which seemed to be in the same condition we left it in, I said to Michael, "If I told her to take her fur coat off coming out of the restaurant, she would have thought I was jealous or something."

"I know, Tina. Even a warning would have been inappropriate. Don't worry about it. I just hope it didn't cost her too much." Deep down inside, I hoped we would find out tomorrow that Dori is not really a CEO but an undercover feature writer doing a magazine article about the perils of wearing fur midtown. But, I knew a hint about that probably would have come up in our conversation about the writers' strike.

When we returned to my apartment, I asked Michael to come up for another cup of coffee and to give him a tour of my studio. He said, "Okay," and ended up staying until four in the morning. I showed him every single fashion that I ever designed, and luckily he seemed intrigued by all of them. It was like his own private fashion show. Our relationship was headed in the right direction, and the whole evening was going to go down in my book.

Chapter 5

The Best-Dressed List

Mary's voice sounded as excited on the other end of the phone as a teenager calling to say she won two VIP tickets to *Jingle Ball*. "You're not going to believe this, Tina, but I just picked up the most recent issue of *Vanity Fair* magazine, and your forest green chiffon design from the 'Spring into Fashion Collection' made the top ten on the Best-Dressed List! It was the beautiful tiered number that Jackie wore to the Daytime Emmy Awards at the Marriot Marquis Times Square. There's a celebratory brunch at 11:30 a.m. in the beauty and fashion director's office tomorrow for all involved. In *Vanity Fair*'s interview with Jackie they inquired who her designer was, and she gladly volunteered the information. She said, and I quote, 'I'm wearing a *Tina Fashion Original* from her newest spring line, which will be hitting stores shortly.' What a plug! And we didn't even pay her to say that!"

"I'll put in a phone call to the office myself to say that we'll be attending. That's just the kind of information I like to hear, Mary. You're such a good secretary for relaying that to me. I'll try to meet you there before noon."

I was pleasantly surprised that the news wasn't related to the typographical error in the promotional advertisement of the Tony Awards sent in by Michael's company. They are going to be held at the Waldorf Astoria Hotel on the twentieth, and the ad somehow had the wrong date. There were rumors circulating around the city that it was a deliberate slipup made by a jealous staffer. That kind of a mistake can lose an audience of readers around Broadway forever, like appliqués blowing off of a dress on a windy corner.

When I arrived at the office of Condé Nast Publications, I shook hands with the fashion director, and she motioned to me to stand next to Jackie so the photographer could snap a group portrait. The guy with the camera was none other than Michael's friend Joc. He was the one that we ran into on the street the other day. Strangely enough, Chris wasn't with him this time. The two are usually a team. Chris must not have known about this gathering. "This Best-Dressed List is a main topic of conversation for at least six months in the entertainment and fashion industries, and it keeps this magazine circulating for at least two," she said. I told her that I was honored to have had one of my designs chosen for the list, and she thanked me for coming to her office to be a part of the upcoming article and celebration.

In the office doorway, a petite girl in her twenties with long, straight, shiny black hair handed me a glass of punch in a pink fluted glass. Mary passed on the beverage and sampled the chicken Caesar salad instead. I slowly sipped the sweet-tasting punch and commented that it was probably the layered tiers of the dress that everyone liked. Mary said, "I think it was the light and airy material of the dress that caused it to be chosen." I knew she also happened to think it was the forest green color that pushed it into the top ten, but a professional designer like myself knows for sure that it is the lines of the design and the way it fits, combined with the two other superficial qualities that make it a winner. I just kept that information to myself. Then I glanced across the room at the girl who handed me the punch and said, "She looks so familiar to me. Do we know her from somewhere, Mary?"

"I think she may be a waitress in the *La Grenouille* Movie Room," Mary answered. "Oh, no," the fashion director said. "She's new to our magazine staff."

Then she asked me if I would mind getting in another photograph, this time with the other nine designers. I quickly moved to the end of the line. I was delighted to be among the ranks of the established designers whose work I grew up admiring. They were an all-important group, but I did not attempt to converse with them, because I simply did not know what to say; nor did they try to converse with me. Everyone had the same contemptuous attitude that day. (The "at times like these we're haughtily snobbish, and it's better to say nothing and just walk away" position.) No doubt, we all learned that while attending classes and fighting our competition way back in fashion design school. An exchange of words among a group of fashion designers can sometimes turn into a heated debate over a matter of taste. As for myself, for some other unknown reason at the present time, I was feeling a bit tongue-tied.

The photographer's light was blinding, and I was in a dizzy state as I swiftly made my way into the ladies' room. The snap on my gray, pinstripe, peplum jacket had popped, and I heard it fall on the floor. I began to feel more than just a little woozy. It was almost like someone had slipped me a Mickey. I told myself that this was a signal to leave before I got caught in a fashion faux pas myself. When I looked in the mirror, my clothes were twisted, and I imagined being chosen for the same magazine's Worst-Dressed List or, worse yet, featured in an article about pill poppers in the fashion industry. That would be the last thing I need right now. I straightened myself up as much as possible and waved to Mary, who was happily chattering with someone in the corner of the room. I had no choice but to escape home to my studio for a full afternoon of sketching and designing. I didn't feel it was necessary to alarm Mary and impose on her perfectly lovely afternoon. She could have the credit for this advance in our success. As long as she was familiar with someone else there, I knew she would be okay.

At home, in my studio, my creativity was running rampant in numerous rough drafts. I didn't know yet if the punch's effect on me was a blessing or a curse. I had an idea one time, which got off to an inauspicious start, because the world wasn't ready to embrace the futuristic turn of one-piece metallic jumpsuits and out-of-space fashion. But after the holidays some people get depressed, and I thought now was the opportune time to try and take this concept to the limit. I was having a lot of fun with it too, in a meet my space family kind of way. It gave me a cosmic escape individually, regardless of whether or not the world will respond in a positive manner. Sometimes, unique and outrageous designs have to be introduced in the name of fashion to shock the older generations and tell today's youth that there are still so many places to go with this. To be a prolific designer you must never cease trying new directions. This one was a real hoot on paper, and I laughed when I began thinking that perhaps I should turn it into a comic strip for the local newspaper.

I didn't regret not striking up a conversation with one of the other designers with whom I posed for the picture. I just wasn't in the mood to talk this afternoon anyway.

I'm really at my most creative side when I want to be myself. I balanced the tea kettle on the stove and delved into my unusual work for the day without encumbering myself with rules or worrying about criticism or the like. I was just a free spirit pretending that an alien was the connoisseur of my work. And if this splendid arrangement of the unusual should end up on the Worst-Dressed List someday in a magazine with a vast circulation, I will laugh even harder, remembering what kind of mood I was in when I invented those creations—not caring in the least who they would impress.

I didn't answer the phone, and I didn't retrieve my mail. I just put in a quick call to Mary to see if she arrived home safely, and then I changed into my long, pink, satin nightgown with a gray hooded sweatshirt, adjusted the fan, and fell off the face of the earth for a while. Deciding that everything else could wait, while I used my imagination, was right, and something I needed to do from time to time.

Even if Michael called, I wouldn't want to go out tonight anyway. In fact, if I was wearing a mood ring it would be reflecting a darker shade of blue—bordering on the color purple. Michael had given me a mood ring once when he was living nearby. It was an expensive ring, made of real silver and rimmed with diamond chips. Some of my other jewelry was simple fourteen- or ten-karat gold given to me by various admirers. Along with being overtly opinionated and an easy target for rivals,

I happen to possess a strange allergy to ten-karat gold, which I discovered when my skin turned green after wearing certain pieces of jewelry.

So many interesting topics in NYC revolve around color. In the past, when I wore fake gold, a green circle would show up on my finger. It used to scare people away, like a mismatched pattern or something. I viewed it as a sign to select certain shades of color carefully in fashion designing. This odd skin response was kind of cool, in a way, though, because it helped me separate the good guys from the cheapskates. I have all of the imitation pieces tucked away in the bottom drawer of my jewelry box— way back in the bottom of my closet.

When I was brand new to the fashion scene and attending various after-parties, I used my mood ring as a conversation piece. I would pass it on to other guests to see if they were feeling emotional that day. I had people easily pinned for an appointment with a psychiatrist at Bellevue. I can't tell you how many times it displayed a pinkish hue for most of the males in the room. It turned totally multicolored when Chris slipped it on during a break at that first magazine cover shoot. He was the most emotionally aroused of all.

When my mind wandered back to my work, I had a quick intermittent flash of fame and fortune. I was sure that the new designs that I had sketched were fun and glittery. But, at the same time, they could be described as provocative and bordering on the ridiculous. Some of the best things in life are done on a whim. The irony of this career is that someone has to hire me to customize a design way ahead of time if they want to be impulsive. My artistic side had emerged in a positive way, and I was beginning to see depth in my field. There was hope for me yet, and I was certain that these new outrageous fashions would sell. But you know what they say: you always have to watch your back in a backless gown. Tomorrow, I will be able to face the world again sensibly. I'll most likely go back to playing the whirlwind game of profession.

Chapter 6

The Exercise Video

The holiday glamour of NYC seemed to have disappeared until next season. The semiformal cocktail dresses and red and green velvet Santa Claus hats had been carefully packed away in zippered bags and plastic boxes with the help of all of the busy people from up north. The added pounds around our waists, however, didn't seem to be going anywhere. The high intake of calories from all of the partying we did was making it hard for us to button our jeans.

It was the week after our New Year's Eve celebration at Planet Hollywood in Times Square, so Lauren, Mary, and I signed up for a workout class to get in shape for the spring. We chose retro aerobics primarily because our schedules didn't allow for a full gym membership, and we preferred exercising to music rather than working out quietly with a personal trainer. We didn't even consider zumba, because the teacher made the last group wear hats to class. Yoga was totally out of the question, because it was only offered in the early morning hours.

Mary had been thrown out of our yoga meditation class years ago because she split her bodysuit, and I went into a fit of laughter. She didn't do it intentionally, but the yoga teacher did not like the interruption. I tried to make Mary feel better by telling her that our personalities called for rejuvenation—not relaxation—and it was cheap material anyway.

We signed up to work out repetitiously with a certified aerobics instructor named Susan. She was thin, blonde, muscle-toned, and excellent at keeping the class moving for a complete hour and a half. Susan uses a careful approach by having everyone take their pulse before the start and then after the warm-up with a stopwatch. "It is, by far, the most important part of our aerobics session," she says straight out. "So that no one drops dead of a heart attack in my class."

Her choice of music varies from 1980s rock 'n' roll to alternative new wave, but it is the perfect balance for a strenuous cardio workout. I once suggested to Susan that she should make an exercise video, for which I would design the clothes, and she surprisingly decided to take me up on the idea. I didn't really want to star in the video; I just wanted to be the designer, but she insisted that the original group be in it, since we were all so good at synchronizing with each other.

My workout fashion idea was retro also, with tie-dyed bodysuits and pink wool leg warmers. Everyone had to wear athletic sneakers and opaque tights. *Tina Exercise Wear* in psychedelic shades was the look I was going for, and the look I believed I was able to pull off, even though we all really wore solid sweatpants and T-shirts to the class on a regular basis.

Mary and Lauren agreed that the back-dated style was perfect for all shapes and sizes, especially for a current workout DVD. I designed the instructor's attire as well. It was a solid version of the bodysuit in lime green, with tight black spandex pants and lime green leg warmers. She was also wearing the same type of cushiony athletic sneakers in white and neon pink. As the certified instructor, Susan was the one who was expected to dress professionally for every class. I thought that in her position, it was only right for her to look a little different than everyone else. Anyone with her endurance has earned the right to stand out from the crowd. Susan had the ability to whip us all into fashion model shape in just a few short classes.

We were in a small gym on the thirteenth floor in a dilapidated apartment building, but there was a nice view from the high-performance sun window. The buildings in NYC don't always have the thirteenth floors labeled, because of that old superstition, so the button on this elevator simply says minigym. "Sometime after class, if the weather is nice enough, we should all go out for a drink of papaya juice to refuel our energy and sit on the roof in the sun for a while—just like we did in the 1980s," Mary said.

"Listen up, ladies," said Susan. "I want you to meet John, the Video Producer. He will be filming our group video, and you all know the moves. Just follow me and listen to his instructions."

John already had his video camera obstructing his face, so it was hard to see what he looked like. I could only tell that he had short black hair, and he was wearing gray sweatpants and brown hiking boots—with multicolored shoelaces that were left untied. I kept thinking that if he trips on those things, the exercise video will move to fashion floor cam.

"Girls, if I zoom in on you, just make it look like you're enjoying the workout. Whatever you do, don't stop moving, and don't look directly at the camera," John said. Then he looked me up and down obnoxiously and said "Tina, I'll highlight your name in the credits for the fashion wardrobe design. If you don't mind, I'll discuss the details with you after the class." I just nodded my head and tried to save my breath as I lined up with the rest of the group. Of course, Mary and I stayed in the back row, and Lauren stole the show up in the front. Even though she's the only one of us who has given birth a few times over, she was actually the best at performing the aerobics moves. She once had surgery for varicose veins in her legs, and she did the leg movements very carefully. In fact, everyone is always telling her that her legs are beautiful for her age, and observant John was zooming in on them the whole time.

As Susan started "Pump it Up" on her stereo boombox, my adrenaline began to flow. You would never need to be on steroids working out to this song. *"Pump it up until you can feel it. Pump it up when you don't really need it."* This fun song was caught between so many others with highly intellectual lyrics: "I Write the Book" being

my absolute favorite as background music in my fashion design studio. *"Even in a perfect world where everyone was equal, I'd still own the film rights and be working on the sequel."* The class kept moving and my mind began to wander some more.

I always thought that my sister, Lauren, should have been a supermodel. Brenda, the one who wears my *Tina Designs*, has long, beautiful legs too. Everyone knows that's the feature that separates the supermodels from the everyday fashion models.

My sports bra was sticking to me, and I was thinking that it is not going to be a prime time to take my worn-out self over to meet with John after the class. I was contemplating sitting out this time, but I didn't want to disappoint Susan. Besides, if my *Tina Fashion Wear* does what it's supposed to, we're supposed to look as cool as cucumbers after the class anyway. The bodysuits are made of breathable material, and they're not supposed to show any signs of sweating. Perhaps I will change the advertising tags for the entire line. "Even the fashion designer looks cool for her workout." I chuckled to myself but refrained from sharing this joke with Mary because I didn't want to ruin the video. It was like retro comedy. When I walked into this gym, my thoughts and language all turned into things from the 1980s; even my warped sense of humor and my vocabulary.

Susan ended the class by winding down to a slower "Wheel In The Sky." We brought our heart rates down to the original lead singer's smooth voice singing "*Wheel in the sky keeps on turnin' I don't know where I'll be tomorrow ...*

"It's over twenty years later, and the wheel is spinning my fashion career out of control. Tomorrow I'll be in my studio working my butt off in my ambitious career."

The whole session was well thought out and planned to increase your pulse rate and then bring it back to normal accompanied by appropriate music played at random speeds. She narrated our stretches, and we all followed along in sequence.

John shouted, "That's a wrap!" in a producer's voice, and we all took a swig from our water bottles. He signaled for me to come out on the roof with him, so I hung my striped aqua towel around my neck and stood next to the bench he was sitting on. I felt jaded, dehydrated, and out of breath, but I understand the importance of faking enthusiasm when it is my part of the work that we are concentrating on. The wind was picking up in high gusts, and I just wanted to hurry back inside. "I know how to spell your last name already, Tina. You're a tad more famous than you let on to be. I'll be frank with you," John said. "I've observed that the *Tina Fashions* label is getting very popular here in NYC."

"My career is moving up," I replied, while still breathing heavily and shielding my eyes from the surge of sand being blown off the roof. "Then I'll cut to the chase. Your first and last name should be great in the credits next to 'Fashion Wardrobe By …' in huge Aspire lettering."

"That's what I thought too," I said. "But not bold lettering, John. Please don't exaggerate my work too much for this. I really want to take a backseat to Susan. After all, it's her video."

"Okay, I'll get to the punch," said John. "Fifty million people ask me to downscale their names in the credits all the time. My real reason for asking you to come out here is to see if you'd like to go on a date or something. Susan clued me in that you might be available."

He doesn't seem to fit into the pattern right now, I thought. *Suddenly the motif has changed. Michael steps back in, my career picks up, and some other guy—with what seems like a promising job and upbeat personality—shows interest in me. He's a thematic element throwing my design off balance in fast motion.* I didn't know what to say. It was like sheer drama and romance tied into a contemporary novel. I really just wanted to get the hell off of the windy roof so I just said yes, and he seemed content with my answer.

Being the free spirit that I am, I knew that I wouldn't want him to pick me up. *An independent fashion designer has to be the one to call the shots*, I told myself like I was rehearsing a soap-opera scene or something. So I asked him to choose the time and the place for the date, and I told him that I would meet him there. "*La Grenouille* Movie Room at eight o'clock," John said. "Peace!"

Now there's a word that I haven't heard in a while, I thought to myself. I inhaled and exhaled some fresh air as I walked back in through the brick doorway to reunite with Mary and Lauren. John really isn't a bad-looking guy at all, but he dresses like a drug-addicted child star. I figured I'd give him a chance. At least he isn't boring. Besides, he has a brazen interest in video production.

I waved to Susan on the way out and she gave me the thumbs up as the three of us headed home to shower and refresh ourselves. We all agreed that the video would probably be a hit—not only on the computer but also right up there on the shelf next to all of the other workout queens. "*A Fashion Designer, A Secretary, And A Mother Do NYC*," Lauren said. "This couldn't be happening to a nicer instructor, either. She'll become a magnet for appropriately dressed fitness freaks. She'll stand out as the opposite of our age group. You know, like skiers who wear blue jeans on the slopes. If John does the DVD cover right and shows her in the lime green getup, she'll make a fortune," I said. It felt really good to be helping someone else out in their climb to fame. I was happy that I made the decision to be a part of the whole thing. I thought it would be a smart move to keep my date with John quiet because I didn't want Mary and Lauren to make a big deal about it.

Chapter 7

The Movie Room

Fashion is to film what culture is to history. Both are dashing displays of tradition and modernism passed down to future generations. People are always searching for new forms of self-expression, and dressing up is the most popular way to do it.

When I arrived at the establishment after eight, John had already picked a small table in the back by the bar. I was glad that he situated us far away from the big screen so that I could distance myself from the action. I had to make a fast getaway once before, from a sense around, because the motion for me was overwhelming. (The design on some guy's tie was much too busy.) John had already ordered a drink for himself and asked me if

I wanted anything. "I'll have an orange juice and club soda to start," I told the waitress, who was wearing a sexy flapper costume from the 1920s.

La Grenouille Cinema Room is actually the name of a sociable lounge in a high-class French restaurant that features silent movies until after midnight and various *a la carte* menus available all hours of the day without reservations. Anytime after twelve o'clock you can walk in, order something to eat and watch a movie. There is no set admission price, but the waitress keeps a tab for your table, and you pay the check when you are leaving. Some people just go there for fancy drinks or luscious desserts. Most people who do go there seem to be old movie buffs who just want to meet other old movie buffs and talk about cinematography. It was nicknamed "The Movie Room" a long time ago by some famous Hollywood actor visiting NYC with ties to the Academy of Film.

"A slightly different scene than filming an aerobics video, wouldn't you say, Tina?" John asked. I nodded my head in agreement. The Hollywood glamour on the big screen was indeed very unlike the casualness of women dancing around and exercising. However, my keen observant nature could tell right away that John liked women in any shape or form doing whatever.

John was dressed in a wrinkled blue shirt with a tan corduroy jacket and a pair of blue jeans. His face was as clean-shaven as a marine's, but his strong-smelling cologne and the deodorant soap he must have showered with lingered in the air. It was completely overpowering, to say the least, and I started to get a headache from it right away. I knew it was a cheap brand of men's cologne. It wasn't even close to the really nice—but discontinued—stash of men's fine fragrances that Michael wears.

I was glad that I didn't spend too much time worrying about what I was going to wear. Considering what was to come later, it wouldn't have mattered that much anyway. The night was foredoomed before I decided on the pencil-thin black jean skirt and black and white striped ribbed turtleneck with black leather boots. This look would probably be more appropriate for an afternoon book-signing event at Barnes and Noble Booksellers. No one was going to be "painting the town red" in this getup. He didn't compliment me on my outfit and I certainly didn't compliment him on his.

Because John was aware that I was in the fashion business, he kept asking me if I liked what everybody else was wearing. As the night progressed and the hour got later, the films and scenes on the screen became more current, revealing, and slightly less glamorous. I no longer felt as if I was the commentator on the red carpet for the pre-Academy Award extravaganza, or a NYC fashion designer advancing my career. I felt like I was the mother of two teenage girls who want to leave the house dressed as cabaret dancers. I didn't want to ruin Susan's chances of getting a good video from him, so I just played along like I was enjoying his company and this kind of thing. I was realizing now that this friendly date put me in a very awkward situation. I just sat there eating my french onion soup with melted gruyére cheese and a crouton in the middle and answered all of his questions all night long. "Well, the black and red spider-man minidress is definitely different and sexy with the black fishnet stockings, but the right high-heeled shoes could have made it more elegant for that particular show," I said. When the live cabaret show came onstage at midnight, I almost couldn't believe it. I had never really stayed late enough to know about the extensive late-night entertainment. The whole night put together was rather amusing.

As he downed his sixth strong drink filled with shelf liquor, John's head spun around in three-sixties all night as if he were possessed. His behavior was totally obnoxious in my presence, zooming in on every single woman in the club with his eyes, not even with a camera. I thought that maybe he had one with a self-timer hidden in his jacket pocket. The waitresses had cute little fringe swinging to the tops of their legs and tassels on their breasts. Most of the clientele were casually dressed males in dark-colored pants and variations of gold-colored ties, with clean white socks and stark white shirts. The other cabaret dancers were wearing nothing but gold jeweled thongs, and even though we were seated in the back, they kept circling our table to sit on John's lap. The last group of dancers were totally nude. I really felt rather uncomfortable in the middle of this situation. I excused myself to go to the ladies' room at least three times during the evening, so as not to intercede between him and his eye candy.

This is not unusual behavior for a fashion designer, I told myself, because I'm into designing clothes that complement the human body. I'm not that into watching so many people not wearing clothes. In my opinion, one article of clothing, like a bow tie, is much more sexy than a totally naked body. I mean, let's leave something to the imagination! I was tempted to tell John what I really thought of him—that his arrogance right in front of me was forcing me to label him a loser. *That's what I like about Michael*, I thought to myself. *When we are out on a date socially, he focuses on me.* The *La Grenouille* downstairs has the reputation of being a very high-class establishment. I knew it could be worse. He could have taken me to a gay hookah bar.

When John pulled out a cigar and told me in slurred speech that he wanted to "Go dutch" with the check, looked at him in disbelief and unwillingly opened my purse. Luckily, I had a higher-paying profession and what I hoped was more class. At least he didn't ask me to pay for his six drinks and frog's legs. I didn't want him to drive home by himself because of his intoxicated state, but I didn't want to volunteer to drive him either for fear he'd make a move on me. So I summed up the situation and called him a cab. Not even a quick kiss on the cheek, and I slammed the door of the taxi. The meter started, and I was on my way home by two o'clock in the morning.

And so John the Video Producer received *Tina the Fashion Designer's* personal award for one of the worst dates she's ever been on. And it was totally unexpected because he seemed like such a nice guy in the minigym. I decided that I wouldn't tell Susan about the miserable evening. It would just be another thing to write down in my book.

Chapter 8

The Worst-Dressed List

Standing out in a crowd by wearing an awful outfit is like being the only giant dressed in sapphire blue in a city full of little people. Everyone gawks at you, and there's no place to hide. Mary was there in person to break the news to me the following week about the scandalous nightmare, which had the potential to turn my whole career upside down. Imagine a fashion designer herself appearing on a Worst-Dressed list for what she was wearing on a calamitous date—and in a photograph with scantily clad cabaret dancers in the background, no less. It turned out that John the Video Producer did not like the fact that I put him into a taxi, and the vicious squirrel had connections to the same magazine accountable for the list. Luckily, we were the ones who attended the party the last time for the previous Best-Dressed List in *Vanity Fair* magazine, and Mary was able to pull my name out of the caption by speaking to the fashion director who so kindly remembered me posing for the photographs with the other designers that day. She also remembered the minute conversation I had with her before I had to leave so suddenly because I could barely speak. She could have been irked by the fact that I snuck out early, but fortunately she did not hold it against me. I later found out that she remembered me from risqué pictures she had found on her desk of me lying on the bathroom floor with my top ripped open—shortly after someone had slipped me the Mickey. Besides, Mary had made her presence known by talking to almost every single person there. We must have made some kind of lasting impression, and fortunately she knows the obnoxious nature of you-know-who. His vicious attempt to sabotage an up-and-coming designer was foiled again. "That is not where Tina's name wants to appear in the prime of her career," said the fashion director to Mary, who promptly relayed the message to me. "That's an understatement," I told her.

Rumor had it that the fashion director of *Vanity Fair* had gone on several dates with John the Video Producer prior to the filming of the aerobics video and that she is an excellent judge of character. She wasn't out to get me. She was out to save my career because she was armed with first-hand knowledge that when John drinks he hits on anybody wearing a skirt. She knows that retaliation is his middle name no matter how gently you let him down. It had to have been someone else on the magazine's staff that physically bypassed magazine policy. Someone else had to have put my name on the list through John's suggestion, and someone else had to have taken those risqué pictures of me that night. Luckily, nothing can be finalized in print until it passes the fashion director's desk first, and the editor's desk second in double-check-system fashion.

"We can relax now, Tina. What might have happened didn't and now you are a little wiser," Mary assured me. "It almost happened in more ways than one," I replied, reviewing the reason I had to leave The Condé Nast Publication's office in the first place. "I had a dangerous liaison for the first time in my life. It was almost as if I was being framed," I said to Mary. "I never told you about the drugged feeling I had after drinking the punch that day, and the fashion faux pas that I surmised would have put me on the Worst-Dressed List even before this had I stayed any longer." Though I never said it out loud, I told myself that this kind of thing would be the exact way to ruin a fashion designer's reputation. Everyone else who made the list might think of it as a boost to their career or a way to be pushed into the celebrity spotlight. But for me—a fashion designer—it would be a permanent stain on my résumé. "That was close," I said to Mary. "But no cigar," I added *using a phrase*, I thought to myself, *of total appropriateness concerning the type of date John put me through and his extreme lack of regard for my feelings at the time.* "Don't bother trying to analyze me. You would have had to have been there."

Mary looked a little confused, but she didn't press me for any further details. Sometimes, the less said the better off the situation will be. In this case, I still had to worry about the way Susan's exercise video was going to turn out, and how Mr. John was going to make all of us look in it. Perhaps I should have sat out and remained behind the scenes. It was another lesson learned, anyway.

"Way to be a great personal secretary, Mary," I said. "What else do you have lined up for me for the rest of the month?"

"Well," said Mary, "this weekend there's the spectacular lingerie fashion show at the Convention Center at the luxurious Hilton Hotel in town. "We'll have to take a limo this time to make our grand entrance," I replied. "If I remember correctly, everyone hops out onto the pink and black carpet and enters through the silver gates."

"Do you remember your outrageous pink lace teddy and ten-thousand-dollar heart-shaped brassiere?" Mary asked. "They are both going to be featured at this extravaganza."

"I was thinking perhaps it would be great fun to match up a pair of letter embroidered sweatpants with a pair of wings to put a unique twist on things. But I'm going to have to dismiss that idea. After that touchy liaison the other night, it would be best if I don't risk taking any more flighty chances with immaturity. It's time to get down to the serious business of fashion designing. Avoiding poor publicity will be my new strategy for a while. Besides, this particular show is supposed to focus mainly on adults and bedroom attire," I chimed. "But, it is almost every girl's fantasy to be a lingerie model or a designer," added Mary. "I'm well aware of that. It was our dream from way back when that landed us here in the first place. That desire plus my degree in fashion design and your knowledge of the business catapulted us straight to the top. I sometimes wonder if life would have been simpler if we had chosen the modeling path."

"Perhaps it would have been, but neither of us has the legs, height, or handwriting," Mary said. "Speak for yourself, Mary," I replied. And we both started to laugh. "I know from experience that it is the supermodels who have to sustain the most abuse in the fashion industry and still come out making it look easy."

Mary shuffled some papers on her lap and pointed out an article on the second page of the newspaper. "*The New York Times* said that the people in charge of the lingerie show may not allow one of the well-known Italian goddaughter's selections to be modeled," she said. "I don't know why—she happens to be a very good designer herself," I replied. "In fact, she became a contender even before I did."

I lowered the tone of my voice to just above a whisper,

as if someone might overhear what I was saying. "I think it has something to do with the approval of her family, and the fact that the setting is NYC. If anything changes, I will gladly let her go first anyway," I explained. "I'm not looking to stir up any trouble here. She's got a true design passed down from generation to generation, which shows a lot of skin. My fashions are just creative originals that are much less revealing anyway."

I led Mary back to the studio, fixed her a cup of tea, and showed her the details of the two designs that the models will be wearing this weekend. It's her job to make sure that the seamstress gets everything right, from the snaps to the bows. They change so quickly it can be nerve-wracking at times. But, Mary and these experienced models will probably be able to pull this off without a stitch. There are several categories in which to compete. My two designs are listed under sexy elegance and playful. The whole thing is being advertised as a sophisticated high-fashion event, and every high-profile designer, model, and celebrity in NYC will probably make an appearance.

Chapter 9

The Hilton Hotel

"Such an array of pretty pastels have been prominently chosen for this fashion show. The silks and satins and glittery designs have outnumbered the leather and lace fad by a mile." Mary was in complete agreement at the concept of the feminine side being the main attraction. "Your two designs were target showcases for this event. The tough black leather sadomasochistic look has been overpowered this year. It's really rather refreshing," she whispered. "Don't let anyone hear you say that, Mary. So many of the older designers are stuck on the notion that it's the only look that really works."

We sat in the second row of seats in the middle of the convention center behind the technicians handling the lighting and the sound system, so as not to upstage the crew and celebrities who had been hosting this for years. The energy set forth by this particular group was overwhelming. It was as if the electricity had been turned on the setting of high alert. One by one the models came out, the designers were acknowledged, the pink spotlights glared, and the music pounded. There wasn't a single pause in the whole program. I must say that it was well planned out and directed. I think the only mistake was a trip by a model when her heel caught the silk train on someone's negligee. She smiled and got up gracefully enough, and some heckler in the audience shouted, "That's what I like!" She just took a bow and flipped her light blonde hair off her shoulders as if it was nothing.

When the white lights came back on for a second, I spied Michael in the second row out of the corner of my eye. I leaned forward to see who he was with and breathed a sigh of relief when I saw Rob sitting next to him. I thought that maybe he was with another woman. Dori was next to Rob wearing some kind of bright purple feathered hat with a giant stick pin by the ear. The lady sitting behind her kept trying to move her head from left to right because the hat was blocking her view.

I pointed them all out to Mary, who promptly inquired about what Dori was wearing on her head. "At least it's not fur, Mary. But I hope that the animal activists don't catch her on the way out this time. We're in the center of dynamic NYC, far from the bird lovers of the world," I said.

The grand finale was a parade of all of the fashion models promenading to "We're Not Gonna Take It," and the crowd went wild! My name was listed in the program along with the other fashion designers, and behind the set was a diamond vision screen flashing the credits for the show. Mary elbowed me when *Tina Fashions* appeared on the screen, but the promoters didn't ask anyone to stand up or come forward. "The Hilton Hotel is a nice venue for such a large crowd," I said to Mary. "Yes, it is. If it wasn't for the construction that's going on right now outside on the streets of the city, it would be ideal," she answered.

When the audience dispersed, the limos pulled up right in front of the main entrance. The unruly crowd of spectators were held back by a corded rope. I was buttoning my coat when I felt a warm hand on my shoulder. It was Michael. "Do you want to ride in the limousine with us?" I asked him. "That would be great," he replied. "I caught a ride here with Rob and Dori, who refused to valet park and decided to steal a spot several blocks away instead of in a parking garage. I tried to tell Rob that it wasn't safe around there, but he insisted," Michael said. Then he whispered in my ear that Rob is completely into having a trophy girlfriend and dancing her around the city on his arm. For that very reason they always park far distances and never take shortcuts. He's not happy unless other guys are giving her the catcall. "You and I both know she's dressing for attention," I added. "And when you dress for attention, you get it." The limousine drove right onto the pink and black carpet, and the crowds cheered as a well-known group of *Victoria's Secret* models pulled away.

Suddenly there was a loud crash and piercing screams from the side where the audience was standing. It was a thunderous noise that shook the entire neighborhood, as if a female King Kong wearing a sapphire blue evening gown had taken a giant step down a city street. A crane collapsed three streets down from the hotel, somewhere in the vicinity of where Rob's car was parked. Rob and Dori had begun their walk back already, and I could see Michael's face turn stark white. "Oh no! I hope they didn't park in the danger zone!" he shouted.

Our limo pulled up next, and we quickly got in and asked the driver to take the back route to where Rob's car was parked. Michael breathed a sigh of relief when he saw Rob and Dori standing on a corner talking to a policeman in full uniform. "Whatever about the car, at least they're all right," Michael said. Dori's purple hat cast a huge dark shadow on the corner of the building. There were orange blockades in a row and red flashing lights on all sorts of emergency vehicles, so we signaled for them to both get in the limo. "The cop says that a strap snapped on the crane and an arm gave way, nearly wiping out every single car on the surrounding street. It was a damn good thing that it wasn't the whole crane that fell. No one was hurt because the construction workers aced the job of securing the space below pretty well. But some city inspector really screwed up. He is going to be in big trouble for this," said Rob.

"It's possible that it was not really an accident. Someone could have been the target for this incident. One of the models could have had a mysterious stalker following her—or, worse yet, someone could have been out to get one of the fashion designers. Someone could have been out to get Tina, for that matter," Michael added.

"That's what one of the firemen said. He also said that I will be able to get my car back in the morning," Rob remarked. "I really hope it's not trashed. It could have been completely totaled."

"Will you listen to me next time, Buddy?" Mike asked. "You and Dori could have been seriously injured or killed, for that matter."

"I'm sorry. Man, I must have been having a Sims moment. You were right about the parking info. It's messed up, isn't it? I guess my mind was on snooze 'cause Dori's such a hot date," Rob answered.

"Do you realize that every time the four of us are together some kind of disaster happens?" I asked. "It does seem that way," Michael replied.

As the driver pulled away, Mary asked him if he could drop her off first. I could tell she was feeling like a third heel or something. She convincingly told us that she had a close cousin coming from out of town and that she had to clean her place up before her arrival. "Thanks a lot, Tina, for everything," she said as she stepped out. "I'll let you know what your next event is tomorrow. You have a small meeting with someone famous at three thirty."

"Okay. Are you sure you don't want to come out with us somewhere tonight, Mary?"

"No, that's been quite enough excitement for me for a single night. Thanks anyway. Later, guys!" Mary said.

Rob suggested DJ Reynolds, an Irish pub just around the corner, and I could tell he couldn't wait to down a bottle of Guinness because of his near mishap tonight. Michael and I went into hysterics to lighten the mood when he suggested that Dori should leave her hat in the car. "It's got a feather on it, Dori. Don't push your luck." I really couldn't believe it when she obediently took it off and set it on the seat in the back. "It's yours for safekeeping," she told the limo driver. "Don't worry, miss, I won't wear it. I might look like a pimp in that thing," he said. "I think you look prettier without it anyway," he added.

Michael asked him to come back in two hours, and he said he would. No one wanted to study the menu so we all ordered fish and chips with vinegar, which was the known favorite. We talked about everything from insurance claims against the city to the music at the lingerie show. Unlike Mr. John, these guys knew better than to try to discuss the actual lingerie fashions in mixed company, even though I am a designer. Our age group doesn't always follow the rule of never discussing politics or religion at the dinner table, and the few gentlemen we have left have their unspoken list of topics never to bring up if you're serious about your date. Depending upon our occupations, most females play along blindly just to keep the mood light. If I was on a date alone with Michael, we certainly would have discussed everything.

Dori kept excusing herself to go to the ladies' room because she had a bad case of hat hair, and her purple spandex dress kept creeping up on her. I could tell she's had better nights, but, I must say, I admire her good-sport let's-chalk-it-up attitude about life. I accompanied her a few times because that's what our generation does, and with the basement restrooms of the city, it's a safer policy to be on guard with a friend. When we came up the stairs the last time one of the waitresses spilled a shot of whiskey on Dori's dress. The heavy drinkers at the bar were having whiskey chasers after each bottle of Guinness. One of the guys asked me if I was in that new nude exercise video on *YouTube*. Then they started to give Dori the catcall, and the two of us just rushed past them to get back to our table. "Now what is it about me that people don't like?" she asked. "Oh, Dori, you know it's not you. It's just a black cloud that's following you for the time being. I hope you don't hold it against NYC. It really is a nice place to socialize. I think the crane accident and lingerie show just brought in an obnoxious clientele this evening." Deep down inside, it was his comment directed toward me that I was worried about.

Dori told Rob about the incident and he immediately jumped up and yelled, "Where are those guys? I'll punch their lights out if they did anything to you." Michael and I just met eyes with each other because we both knew that Rob was not the violent type, nor could he match up to the smallest lightweight in a fight. "Simmer down, Rob," Michael said. "It's the first time I've ever seen any aggression like that from my good buddy. The last thing we need is a headline tomorrow morning about a bar brawl involving the four of us. It would be bad for our public relations firm and horrendous publicity for *Tina Fashions*. Let's just pay the check and leave while we still have our heads about us."

Michael picked up the tab again, which came to about ninety-five dollars including the tip, and we all got back in the limo for a smooth ride home. None of us did any more talking. Dori put her hat back on, which was still in good shape, and Michael put his arms around my shoulders. Although I am not easily rattled by too many things, it felt nice to be in this comfortable secure moment with him after all of the things that went on. When Dori and Rob got out, Michael said that Dori might have to get a higher-paying job if she's going to continue to date Rob. "So far their relationship has cost her a fur coat and dry cleaning for her dress."

"He almost lost his car too," I added. "They could have lost their lives," Michael said. "I think they both lose their sense of reasoning when they're together. That's the biggest price of all. Perhaps they are discovering that they're really in love. That's the thing that's going to be the most costly in their relationship."

Actually, it was my relationship with Michael that I was starting to feel good about. He rolled up the tinted glass between us and the driver, put on some low music, and we both enjoyed the twenty-minute ride home. It was about four in the morning. I kissed him goodnight and waved to the driver, remembering that I never paid him for the transportation. I didn't worry, though, because I knew Michael had it covered.

Chapter 10
The Meeting

The next day my energy level was so low, I felt like a fizzling sparkler that had to be relit because it was left out in the rain all night. My business meeting was supposed to be at three thirty, but I was running so late that I called Mary to reschedule until four o'clock. The business at hand happened to be with a famous New Yorker who was nominated for an award for best actress for a supporting role. It was to be presented at the Golden Globes in two months. Instead of being held in Hollywood, California, this year, the Hollywood Foreign Press Association and the organizers of the award show chose NYC's own Tavern on the Green for the event.

This particular celebrity was referred to me via the

private gossip chain of a dead designer in NYC. As soon as he passed on, she called and asked me to be her new designer. I told her that it would be my pleasure, and we lightly breezed over her likes and dislikes. I then asked her to come in to my studio to look at a book of my professional designs. I told her that she could flip through the book to see if she would like an existing *Tina Fashion*. Then she would have the option to have me design a brand new *Tina Original* to call her own.

My friend Daniel from graphic design helped me put a book together when my career started to move forward. He did a great job with it too—using a three-inch clear-view binder and excellent computer graphics. In fashion design class they advise you never to let potential clients see your original sketches or artwork. I'm from the old school anyway. Most of my original sketches look like penciled-in stick figures wearing triangular skirts from my younger days. However, even songwriters scribble original lyrics on cocktail napkins, so I've heard it's not a bad way to be. When your creative side wants to emerge you have to let it, no matter what the circumstances are. Daniel gave my book of samples the professional look it needed. I am always proud to have people look at it. He is much more into business than I am and much less into the arts.

The actress, Melissa Tray, was a thin dark-eyed beauty. Since most of my fashions are modeled by slender people like her, I suggested that we go with something unadulterated, which would be most unusual for her age group. My standard fee for a new design was three thousand dollars. I told her that once she signed the contract it could not be reneged. She didn't blink at the price, nor did she think twice about signing the contract. But that would have been hard to tell anyway, because the conversation was taking place over the phone.

"As you already know, my former designer passed away this year," Melissa said. "He told me himself, when he was on his deathbed, to keep you in mind as the next fashion designer to be in the spotlight. He had seen your work at a summer fashion show and had come down with AIDS right after. Of course, he knew that he had already made his mark in the world of fashion, and he didn't want me to be left out in the cold," Melissa told me.

To make a long story short, Melissa is a bombshell, and looking good is important to her. In fact, she's been in the news for her fashion sense many times, and the people of NYC know her well since she was born in Brooklyn. She was as much a pleasure to have in my studio as a life-size mannequin displaying my latest work of art.

"Tina, babe, design something classy, sophisticated, and elegant, so that I feel good at the podium next to all those younger blondes. I don't want to look like I'm in the wrestling ring for the Golden Globes. With the right dress, I'll be able to have fun whether I win or not. I'd like a sexy low neckline since this freakin' bod has helped me snag lots of good roles." She looked down and smacked her butt, and I just laughed. "Electric blue taffeta is what I had in mind—to the floor with a tissue bottom," I said. "How does that sound to you?" I asked her. "Listen, I've seen your work, and I trust you. Besides, if it's not right, we have two months to play with the design, Melissa replied. "I've been dressing down too much lately and I want to turn it all around. This is a great time for me," she said.

I was getting the feeling that a tornado of good luck was blowing my way right here in NYC. This rich, famous Brooklyn-born actress with lots of money was going to use me, Tina, as her own personal designer. She bared all in her most recent movie, but she isn't really the type to do that, if you know what I mean. She is the exact one who can bring Hollywood glamour back to NYC. That's what movie goers expect from actors at an award show. If I do this right, the next screenplay written will be titled *Tina the Fashion Designer Does NYC*.

"Don't worry, Melissa. I'll do my best to work with you. I'll have Mary set up another appointment, and I promise I won't keep you waiting next time. We were out late last night and in the area of that crane accident," I told her. "Oh, I heard about that. I used to go to that lingerie fashion show at the Hilton all the time, but this year I had to be in Los Angeles. Don't worry about being late. It's virtually impossible for me to keep to a schedule in this business anyway. I confess. I like some time to myself far away from the paparazzi. I love acting, but I'm sick of being followed. I used to run into the middle of a group of people, but not anymore." She stopped talking for a minute to answer her cell phone.

"Oh, yeah, here are two tickets to the Golden Globes in the Crystal Room at The Tavern on the Green in March. You know, the glass-enclosed catering hall in the heart of Central Park. Don't ask me why they'll be taking place here in NYC in March, instead of Hollywood in February. But, stranger things have happened. Like some people thought they saw a ghostly figure in an evening gown floating down the streets of NYC last night. Anyway, you can bring Mary or someone else. You decide," Melissa said. I thanked her and walked out with her to the street, where a group of fans and photographers had gathered. As she made her way into the back of the white stretch limo, she stopped to sign a few autographs anyway. That, as we already discussed, is not a common practice in these days of pushy paparazzi. The actors and actresses just want to get the hell out of there nowadays.

"What a nice person," I told Mary when I went back upstairs. "The richest ones are usually such bitches that they take the fun out of creating a design. She just makes everything such a pleasure. I'll enjoy working with her."

I offered the ticket to the Golden Globes to Mary, but she politely declined, saying that she had that vacation planned for the month of March at her timeshare in the U.S. Virgin Islands. "You should invite Michael, Tina. The two of you are heating up the fire again, I can tell. The

Tavern on the Green is nice inside too, and I'm sure you'll get a scrumptious dinner and then a chance to intermix with celebrities. It will be a momentous occasion and a chance to see your work shine if she wins. Maybe she'll thank you in her acceptance speech, Mary said.

"These are the types of perks that I always wanted in my fashion designing career," I told Mary. "Do you want to quit early? I'd really like to go home and fall into bed," I added. "I'm always willing to take the rest of the day off, Tina. The work will still be here in your studio tomorrow—along with all the blank pages of paper ready to be filled with a crowd of wild designs. But, let's go to the minigym tonight anyway. The time has come for Susan to show us all her newly released exercise video by John the Man," she replied. "Okay, I'll meet you there later."

Chapter 11

The Bomb

There was a black cloud hanging over the NYC skyline and a tense feeling in the air as I made my way home to sleep for just an hour. When the boom of a box truck woke me up after only a few minutes of rest, I changed into gray flannel-lined sweatpants and a white T-shirt. The imprinted phrase "No sweat," across the back, drew some attention from the truck driver who was making the delivery downstairs. "I'm working up a sweat, sweetheart," he shouted, as I started to jog toward the minigym. I smiled and proceeded to quicken my pace.

I was as eager to see the final production of the exercise video as a new fashion model waiting to see what she will be assigned to wear for her debut on the runway.

I imagined the worst camera angles of my butt doing the warm-ups. I hoped that there would not be any vitriolic comments dubbed in by you-know-who. As vengeful or spiteful as Mr. John could be, I really hoped that he was going to show a proclivity for professionalism in the video for Susan's sake. I had a slightly nervous feeling that any misappropriate moves or bloopers would be emphasized in my general direction.

"Let this be a reminder, *Tina the Fashion Designer*," I said aloud to myself in the elevator, "to stay behind the scenes in everyone else's work but my own. And never date an offensive, scurrilous womanizer who is in charge of filming you exercising—especially one as bold as the print on that guy's jacket."

The elevator door slowly opened, and I joined Mary and Lauren sitting Indian-style on a mat in the back. Mary was working on her posture by pressing her back up against the wall. Lauren's matted face just looked like she had been crying about something. I could read my sister like a book, and I could tell that an argument must have taken place at home. The timing was bad, so I didn't press her for a reason for the tears right then. Besides, I knew that eventually I would get the whole story.

"I am so pleased with the results of the video," Susan said as she made her way to the front of the room. "Mr. John, unfortunately, could not be with us tonight because he is not feeling well."

"He's probably nursing a hangover," Mary whispered

to me as she muffled a laugh. "Or hanging out with a nurse," I replied.

Susan was so pleased and said, "This is the most cosmopolitan exercise video I've ever starred in. You are the most in-shape and best-looking group I've ever had the pleasure to lead." *But then again*, I thought to myself, *Susan always manages to find a way to accentuate the positive. Her outlook on life is heartening.* I figured out at that moment that John didn't make us look bad at all—at least not in her copy of the DVD.

The class was quiet after she hit play, but she paused the video a few times to point out her favorite parts. The *Tina Exercise Wear* was great on everyone—especially Susan—who absolutely looked radiant and in charge. The class knew it too, and our instructor's eyes were beaming like the synchro com-reversed font lights on Broadway. When the credits rolled, they were a little different than John said they would be at our first meeting on the windy roof. I actually liked the wording better his way, since it was Susan's video anyway. I started to feel a little guilty about implying that he would mess it up on purpose. Maybe it was someone else who tried to put my name on the Worst-Dressed List. I scrapped my original opinion of him. He really wasn't all bad, and he has made Susan the happiest woman on the planet. We all applauded at the end, and Susan made us run through it once as if we were regular people who just purchased the video, and we were all exercising in front of our DVD players.

"You'll be toning people up all over the USA," Mary said. Susan flashed a smile as bright as the sun in your eyes when you drive out of the Midtown Tunnel. Then she thanked everyone for participating. She took me aside to personally thank me for the wardrobe. "It was so much fun to do this," I told her. "Your next role will probably be on *Dancing with the Stars*."

"Oh, by the way, Tina. How was your date with John?" she asked me on the side, as she began handing out the complimentary DVDs. I wistfully told her that I was serious with Michael, and that I didn't think I'd be dating John again ever.

In the elevator, I asked Lauren why she'd been crying. She said, "I found Jimmy in the *La Grenouille* Movie Room last night, and he was sitting at a table with John the Video Producer and two other women. I didn't know what to do at first so I left without him seeing me. When he got home, I asked him where he had been, and he told me he was at the ESPN Sports Bar in Times Square. You know, the one with the big flat screens everywhere. He lied and said that he was watching an Islander/Ranger game that was taking place at Madison Square Garden. Do you remember the old Gorton fisherman jerseys that the Islanders used to wear? Anyway, it's not the fact that he was at the *La Grenouille* that bothered me—despite the cabaret dancers—as much as the fact that he lied to me straight to my face. I told him to go live with his brother for a while, and he packed his bags and left."

"Those jerseys were strange. I always thought that they should go back to wearing the old ones. What were you doing in the Movie Room in the first place, Lauren?" I asked. "I went down to the twenty-four/seven convenience store on the corner for a pack of cigarettes. They're over seven dollars a pack now, and I saw the yellow sports car parked right in the front. You can't miss that thing. It's easier to spot than someone wearing a red veil at a wedding. I think Jimmy originally bought it to keep track of me. You know, I never went out at night when the children were little, but now that they're older I'll take a walk every now and then. We have a security guard in the front of our building, and NYC doesn't feel as dangerous as it used to. Oh, what am I going to do, Tina?" she cried.

"Lauren, chill out for a minute. You'll figure out what to do. You think you have a slight chance to work it out, don't you?" I asked. "I'm not sure that I even want to work it out anymore," Lauren replied. "I've had a touch of the single life recently, and I must say that I kind of like it. I know I'll be all right no matter what happens. It's the rest of my family that I'm worried about."

"Sometimes you don't know what you have until it blows right out of your hands," I said to Lauren. "You used to seem very happy when you were out together as a family. I know Jimmy's acting like an idiot. Just do me a favor and see a marriage counselor again. You have to give it the old college try. And most of all be careful what you wish for." She just nodded, gave me a hug, and headed for home. I didn't know if that was the right advice to give to Lauren, but right now Jimmy is the one with the secure job, health insurance plan, benefits, and free parking.

I had to take the long way back to my studio because a crowd was gathered outside the Broadway play *Young Frankenstein* at the Hilton Theatre, the Live Nation Venue. I spotted the famous actress getting into the limo outside the theatre, but she had already changed from her costume. When Michael and I saw that play recently, we had great seats until a tall man with a top hat sat in front of us.

In my own mind, I had changed my opinion of John the Video Producer back to the original one, even though I knew I couldn't fault him for my brother-in-law's behavior. Then I had a revelation. It suddenly struck me that maybe it was my brother-in-law who tried to put my name on the Worst-Dressed List at *Vanity Fair*. Maybe he didn't like the fact that Lauren was dressing up, attending fashion events, and socializing with me. Lauren is starting to look really good lately. All of the exercising is getting her back in shape, and she is starting to look like she had a professional makeover or something. She is wearing some of my past designs and fixing herself up before leaving the house. She keeps telling me things like, heterosexual guys like women who flaunt it—but those same guys do not like their wives to have social lives.

"Almost every woman in NYC today manages to dress for success—while simultaneously keeping their families looking like fashion plates as well," she told me. "But Jimmy won't let me have it. When I dress up, he doesn't want anything to do with me. And when I dress down, I don't feel good about myself. If I make the kids dress up, I'm a butt-whipping mother, but if I make them dress down, I'm an uncaring one. If I let the kids dress the way they want to, everyone comes out looking like a cabaret dancer, and strange guys out there in Internet world think they're older than they really are. I don't know, Tina. If I keep this little gold wedding ring on my finger, who knows what we'll all come out looking like."

It was all starting to come together now. I decided to keep the accusation against my brother-in-law to myself in case I'm wrong. But, at the same time, I was starting to get a knot deep down in my stomach. Maybe the cabaret dancers are out to ruin me, my career, and my family.

Chapter 12
The After-Party

The political aspects of the fashion business were standing as firm as mannequins on all of the morning talk shows and in almost every monthly periodical. The controversial topic of appropriate attire for the workplace wasn't going anywhere. *Vanity Fair* magazine was having yet another cover shoot for a teenage singer whose father slash manager had consulted me about a tasteful *Tina Fashion* that would possibly help to elevate her career. Her latest cover shoot, which was bordering on the obscene, almost sparked a fashion riot. It seems the previous photographer had talked her into showing too much, and the rest of the world, including her father, did not like it. She was supposed to keep her good girl image.

The wraparound toga look, with nothing underneath, just didn't cut it. Shortly after, there was a bad review of a racy concert. "She needs help fast," her father told me, "before she spirals out of control." Without giving it too much thought, I brilliantly came up with a sexy, young, chic—yet classy, sophisticated, and completely modest— outfit for her to wear, with my *Tina* label insignia on it. I must say, I was paid nicely for it.

My outfit featured a denim miniskirt with a white tiered eyelet-lace white blouse accessorized by thigh-length boots. The outfit combined with dynamite photography and superb lighting by Michael's friend Chris, with whom I had reconnected in front of the library that day, resulted in a unique cover that portrayed the young singer's zest for fashion and for life in general. It looked beautiful on her. I was pleased, she was pleased, her father was pleased, and the magazine was pleased. Pleasing so many people at the same time is not an easy thing to accomplish in one day anymore, so we all attended an after-party to celebrate.

Right away, Chris walked up to me with a drink in his hand. "Congratulations," he said. "The clothes you designed for her should do wonders for her image. And, Tina, you look like a professional fashion designer with a soaring career—sporting a body that won't quit."

I was wearing a dressy navy blue and cranberry suede pantsuit with a short zippered jacket. It was a two-piece and two-toned suit with a feminine flair because the pants flared out like bell-bottoms, and both pieces hugged me at the waist. The jacket had a silver zipper up the center and a wide-lapel collar.

"Well," I answered, "Chris, you're always so generous with your favorable comments. To tell you the truth, I'm not used to being the one that's being observed. But thank you. You're looking pretty good yourself, and your lighting was phenomenal. There wasn't a glare in her eyes or a shadow near her youthful face."

"Have you seen Michael these days?" he asked. "We took a limo ride home from the Hilton Hotel the night of the lingerie show and the crane accident and that was really the last time I saw him," I explained. "Oh, I'll have to call him. I read in the local police beat in *The New York Times* that all the cars, including Rob's car, which survived the crane accident, were vandalized the same night anyway because the cops wouldn't let the people through the blockades to retrieve them," he answered. "You're kidding me," I said, and couldn't help but laugh. There was something funny about Rob and Dori's streak of bad luck. "He must have shattered a mirror or something," I said. "Rob and Dori happened to be in the limo with us that night as well. In the past few times they've been out with us, they've had a series of unfortunate events. Technically, they could both be huddling under an open umbrella of bad luck indoors for seven more years." This time it was Chris who laughed. "I know. I already heard about the fur coat disaster." He met eyes with me as if he was searching for something else that I couldn't figure out, so I excused myself to go to the bathroom.

When I came out, Chris had the young singer cornered by his lighting equipment, and he was telling her how pretty her outfit was. I avoided the punch this time, and I kept a keen eye on who was serving the refreshments. I didn't want to be slipped a Mickey at this after-party. Everything was going too well. The singer's father came over to thank me. I surmised that he was around my age, but he seemed different than the guys living and working in NYC. He had shoulder-length brown hair and a goatee and lived in a pair of blue jeans, prairie shirts, and a black leather jacket. He didn't use big vocabulary words, but spoke in a very laid-back, casual kind of way. This was probably because he was experienced in the music scene here, as well as in California. Even though his way of speaking wasn't ostentatious, you could tell that he was very smart. He had a very refreshing carefree personality and a nice, polite way about him. I told him that he did an excellent job of passing his music experience down to his daughter. Then I told him that it was going to hurt me to say this, but his own promotional manager did a great job of making him famous by helping him to break into the business with one great but lame song. He laughed and said that he did an even better job promoting his daughter's career by choosing me as her fashion designer. He told me he would keep me in mind for the future, and judging by the way things were going, we all looked like we had a fun, bright road ahead of us.

After a little more conversation, I said good-bye and went home to work on Melissa's design. The studio was a little cool, so I turned up the heat using the new thermostat that the handyman had installed. I was home when he came in to fix it, and he was appropriately dressed in white carpenter overalls and a black, long-john shirt. He had a hammer in his pocket as a prop, but he never used it; and he was singing "*21st Century Breakdown*" with iPod headphones attached to his ears. The black bandana hanging from his pocket completed his typical handyman attire. "I don't think that's the song that's playing on your iPod," I told him. But he pretended not to hear me.

The landlord of the building had put the order in immediately on October fifteenth, when I first called to tell him I was tired of having to wear a sweatshirt over my nightgown. I was having trouble maintaining a comfortable temperature in my studio apartment and couldn't decide what to wear to bed. It was a brand new and expensive heating system that had just been installed in our building; but, so far, it was not a great improvement from the old-fashion radiators. Although money is no longer a worry of mine, I still have to be concerned about skyrocketing oil prices, bathrobes, and cover-ups here in NYC—just like the people who own the big houses on Long Island.

I sketched five possible low heart-shaped necklines before coming up with one suitable for Melissa Tray's figure. Then I sketched a few variations for the bottom of the gown. One design flared out only where it touched the floor by the hem, one flared out from the knees, one had satin ribbon trim on the bottom, one had pleats all the way down, and one had a crinoline so stiff it could be a mermaid's fin. I finally decided on the one that flared out from the knees down with the tissue-style bottom. It looked lovely when I shaded it in with an electric blue pastel, especially in front of my painting of the NYC skyline. She had to have free movement in the leg department to easily walk on stage. There's nothing worse than having a dress too tight to walk in. I remember one time I was wearing a pencil-thin gabardine skirt to an extravagant fundraiser pageant. I had a lot of trouble trying to get off of the plush sunken-in sofa they ridiculously chose for the panel of judges to sit on. This design looks like a masterpiece and will be comfortable to wear.

I decided to call Melissa myself to set up an appointment, considering I was late the last time. "Melissa, the design is beautiful, and I can't wait for you to see it. It would be best to meet in the office again so no one else gets their hands on the design. Unless you want to dress incognito and go somewhere for lunch on me."

"No way!" she replied. "It was freakin' crazy outside in the city last time! Probably 'cause my new movie is such a blockbuster. I'll grab a cup of coffee or tea in your office to get a sneak preview of your *Tina Fashion*, and we'll see if it's right for me. I'll meet with you tomorrow so the seamstress can get to work on it right away," she replied. "No problem. Three thirty will be great. I think you're going to like it," I told her.

As soon as we hung up, the phone rang, and it was Michael on the other end. We had a lengthy conversation about all of the things that have been going on since we saw each other last. I told him about Melissa Tray and the Golden Globe tickets. I told him about Chris, the singer, and the after-party. I told him about Lauren and her problems with Jimmy and, finally, about Susan and the exercise DVD. He questioned me about John the Video Producer, and I decided that honesty would be the best policy under the circumstances. I blurted out to him about the awful date and everything that followed. Michael turned very serious and said, "It serves you right, Tina, for going out with another guy socially and not even in the name of business. Well, in a way I know that you were promoting Susan's exercise video. You'd better watch it next time, babe. Any number of things could have happened if you drove him home."

Little did he know that a number of strange things did happen already. But I drew the line at telling him everything. "My magnified butt in the video would have been almost as bad as a tarnished reputation, Michael. I learned my lesson, anyway. So, will you come to the

Golden Globes with me in March or what?" I asked him. "Of course, Tina. I would never miss the Golden Globes with you. Even if someone paid me not to go, or if I ripped my pants, or if my tie got caught in an elevator door, I would still find a way to be there with a smile on my face. How about dinner and a movie tonight?" he asked. "Just the two of us for a change. I'll pick you up at eight o'clock."

Chapter 13

The Secret

Indecision about what to wear that night crept into my closet like a pair of extra-tight boy shorts underneath a polyester skirt. I was just slipping into my black satin blouse and powder blue jeans when Michael came to the door. "It's a casual date, right?" I asked him. "I wouldn't want my career to plummet because of a poor choice of an outfit again."

Michael held his hands up as if he was framing my face with his fingers. "Tina, you look great. The only thing I might do is put a replica of you on a sixteen-by-eighteen-foot billboard in Times Square or on the side of a bus," he said.

"You're an excessive flatterer now too. You and Chris

must have rubbed off on each other in public relations class, management class, photography, or charm school. He always has something nice to say when I meet him too."

"We both decided long ago that dispensing compliments on beautiful women is a succinct way to a good relationship. The year after college he foisted thousands of admirable praises on the right girl, and they ended up getting married. I later found out that she left him for a French Canadian foreign exchange student who was even more of a smooth talker."

"I'm glad he didn't give up his enchanting personality. I have an eager desire to match him up with someone I know. He seems like he knows how to treat a woman," I said. "You're a good judge of character, Tina. I've often thought of matching him up with someone myself."

Michael was also wearing blue jeans again, but with a white thermal hooded sweatshirt under a charcoal corduroy blazer. He looked great, in a natural, classy, intellectual, romantic, athletic, rock 'n' roll—yet professional—kind of way, without the chemicals, of course. No matter what he had on, he always looked clean and neat and male-model stylish. That kind of style lives on forever, and I felt damn lucky to be reunited with him at such a good time in my life.

We caught the nine o'clock showing of *The Notebook*, based on that wonderful romance novel with the same name. Then we went for some Greek food at Nikos' Mediterranean Grill. We shared a fantastic Greek salad adorned with feta cheese, black olives, and fresh cucumbers. (Green, black, and white—like a spring-fling model wearing a green dress and reading a newspaper.) Then we both had gyros on homemade pita bread. I asked the waiter, who was dressed in creased black dress pants and a white cotton shirt, if he would substitute onion sauce for the yogurt sauce, because I'm allergic to active yogurt cultures. He said that it wouldn't be a problem, and then Michael ordered his gyro the traditional Greek way.

"What happens to you if you have active yogurt cultures, Tina?" Michael asked me. "Don't you remember? I get a reaction that looks like polka dots on my body," I replied. "That's odd. I always thought they looked like puffy, misplaced shoulder pads."

We headed to the Starbucks three doors down for iced caramel macchiatas with whipped cream, but we didn't sit down. We just talked, sipped our drinks, and walked briskly by the dressed-up mannequins in the window of a shop along the brightly lit avenue. "The row of stores seemed to be lined in a significant order. Satin nightgowns, jeans, and fancy dresses, *Mont Blanc* pens, and shoes, shoes, and more shoes. That's what life is about," I said to Michael.

"No, Tina. Life is about ice cream, and I consider myself to be a connoisseur on the subject. But this place is second best for frozen treats in NYC," Michael said.

I threw my cup in the recycle bin by mistake instead of the garbage, and I was guilty of leaving it there, and it bothered me. But the scene I captured next rendered me motionless like a wax figure in Ripley's NYC. Out of the corner of my eye, I saw Jimmy, Lauren's husband, hailing a taxicab with a black-haired girl on his arm. She was dressed in one of those flapper costumes with the fringe dangling, and she had pin-straight hair nearly to her waist. I quickly figured out that she was the dancer from the *La Grenouille* that he had been caught cheating with last time. When she bent down to get in the taxi, I could see a tattoo of a black rose on her lower spine. She was a *Girls Gone Wild* type, and I guessed that she could be no more than twenty-five years of age. I knew I'd seen her at least three or four times before, but I couldn't remember where else I saw her. When he hopped in the cab they zoomed away from the curb, skidding slightly on the sand in the street that was left over from the last snowstorm. Somehow I managed to observe every detail of the heart-wrenching scene without being noticed by them, and I got really upset.

"Tina, what's the matter?" Michael asked me. "You look like you've been stunned by a Taser." I didn't want to tell him, but since I had given him a preview of Lauren's marital troubles beforehand on the telephone, I reluctantly described the indecorous occurrence that just took place, and I pleaded with him to keep this a secret until it was the right time to tell my sister. The rest of the night was doomed for me, and I was mad at the uncaring, neglectful behavior of my brother-in-law and the bleak picture of the future state of Lauren's marriage. Jimmy was a glutton for punishment to wear a surfeit of lust on his arm in the very own city where his family lives and works. I was disgusted and upset that he had ruined a perfectly enjoyable evening for me and Michael.

"I know he didn't see me, but the quick getaway was far from innocent. I'll have to weigh the consequences and see if and when it's appropriate for me to tell Lauren."

Then Michael said, "Tina, I think it's as good a time as any to tell you my important news." I knew him too well, and I guessed that he just wanted to get my mind off of this deplorable situation. "My work on the Winter Gala is coming to a close, and generally speaking that would mean my having to leave NYC. However, the corporate headquarters for my public relations firm is relocating back to NYC, and they have offered me the permanent opportunity to do the same. So, to make a long story short, I am moving back to my old apartment here in NYC. The PR work for the Winter Gala's production company and the New York Public Library will be my main accounts, along with some other significant ones involving public relations work for NYC. You'll be able to display your fashion designs for me all the time now," he said excitedly. I just threw my arms around his neck and hugged him, nearly ripping the sleeve on my blouse. "We'll have all kinds of occasions to dress up for in the future," I said.

Deep down inside I felt euphoric and depressed at the

same time. Happy about the good time we were having in our lives but heartbroken about my sister's situation. "Well, it's really no big surprise to me that there are snares in life sometimes, just like in my profession. Lauren and Jimmy will either work it out, or they won't. And if they don't, there are a million eligible bachelors in NYC that Lauren can date. She can always pick out a gown and go on *Dancing with the Stars*," I told Michael.

By now the two of us were feeling jaded emotionally and physically, so we called it an early night. "Tina, if you're not sick of me already, Rob and Dori wanted to go to the Gotham Comedy Club with us tomorrow night. Are you in?" he asked. "Sure," I said. "I could probably write a whole comedy routine myself about our double dates alone."

"If your specialty wasn't fashion designing, you'd be very good at doing stand-up. I'll pick you up at eight thirty. There's dinner, a two drink minimum, and a very strict 'No tank top' rule."

Chapter 14

The Comedy Act

The next day my only contact (in the business sense) was a quick meeting with Mary about some upcoming events and ordering some sketching supplies and, of course, the meeting with Melissa in the afternoon. She gave me the two tickets for the Golden Globes, and I told Mary to keep them in a safe place. She suggested that we may want to put them under lock and key. I never mentioned anything about seeing Jimmy the night before, nor did I try to call Lauren to converse. I thought I'd give it a few days before intervening in her life any further. Besides, bad news usually travels faster than a button popping off the horizon here in NYC.

Melissa had her usual entourage waiting outside by

the limo. She looked out at the crowd underneath the window as she drank her coffee and told me that she likes to call them her "people paparazzi." Then she said that the sapphire gown I had created specifically for her was absolutely beautiful. "I just want to float around NYC in it," she told me. She chose the exact bottom that I did out of the original five and the low neck that would show off her sexy figure. "You're such a pleasure to deal with in this fashion business. I'm really very happy with the intricate details of the design," she said. "Maybe one of the photogs will catch a good picture of you wearing it," Mary interjected. "We can have it blown up into a hologram image," she said. "Like the sign with the band: A Whirlwind Profession."

On a daily basis, Melissa lived in blue jeans and velour sweatshirts. Today she happened to be wearing a black one with a white lace tank top underneath. Her velour jacket looked comfortable to travel in, and it had a hood. Even though I didn't design it, I would have liked it for myself. "Thanks for the tickets, Melissa. Michael and I are looking forward to attending the award show and seeing you on stage wearing my *Tina Fashion*. By a slim chance, even if you don't win, you're sure to be a rave in that dress," I told her.

"Tina, I'll be sure to give you the credit you deserve during the preshow and anywhere I can fit it in. Here's the money I owe you. Now we just have to make sure they fix it right. I wouldn't want a hook to fall off or any other wardrobe malfunction. If I drop the damn award, I might rip the seam and moon everyone." Mary and I laughed at her joke, and we walked with her outside to the limo to protect her from the cheering fans.

When we were once again alone in the office, I did elicit the information to Mary about Michael moving back here and about our forthcoming date with Rob and Dori. "You're welcome to join us at the Gotham Comedy Club too, Mary. We can fit more people at our table there." Mary declined, saying that she had made plans with one of the girls from the concert. They were going to a sushi bar downtown, and I think she was looking forward to possibly hooking up with her young male friend from the warm-up band. "You lucky designer you," said Mary. "It seems like things are looking up. It will be nice to have Michael back here in NYC. Melissa's funny, isn't she? Let's just say she's blunt and very down-to-earth!"

I was wearing an expression of approvable on my face, and Mary returned a mysterious smile. Then I told her that I was going to go home to plan my own outfit for tonight's date. I didn't need any jokes about a shoddy blouse or cheesy dress by some entertainer with a microphone in front of me. I had made a silent vow to myself never to be lazy with my own apparel again. Therefore, I had in mind to wear a burgundy gauze dress with a big, wide, brown leather belt and brown leather boots. Underneath, I was going to wear a navy blue bodysuit with lace just at the top, sort of like the one

Melissa had on. It would be both comfortable and sexy, which is how most of my *Tina Fashions* are described. Some of the young rookie designers are sedulous copiers of my work in trying to capture those qualities, but I don't think they really know how to combine the two. I have always had a natural inclination to design fashions how I like to dress. And if I may say so myself, it seems to be working. Melissa's kind words had given me an ego today that kind of put me in a better mood.

Michael was prompt, as usual, and he looked scrubby and cute because he didn't have time to shave. I don't know why, but he thinks that makes me want to kiss him even more. He was wearing khaki pants with ten pockets and a forest green fleece, zippered only to the chest.

When we arrived at the comedy club, Rob and Dori had chosen a great table far away from a group of sleazy hecklers sitting in the front. Every time a comedian would tell a joke they would ad-lib a comment or cough or spill a drink. One guy had a deep-throated laugh, as if he had been a heavy smoker for years.

We ordered some light food and our two beverages and laughed through all the jokes about ethnic groups, different religions, heavy people, thin people, and some of life's quirks. It was all rather amusing, and no one was really offended because included in the three acts there must have been a joke about everyone under the sun. I finally caught on, after watching the hostess seat people in the dimly lit bar, that there was a lesbian side and a straight side. The laughs came from different corners all night.

Dori looked cute too in a tan suede dress with sheepskin fur across the bottom and cuffed around the sleeves. It had a southwestern Indian flair, almost like what Pocahontas wore in the history books. For some reason it looked good on her, not really like a costume or anything. Rob had a few drinks in him, and he kept trying to snuggle up to her. He was saying things like, "Where's your papoose?" and getting really silly. Michael turned to me and whispered, "Something's wrong with Rob. I've seldom seen him let his hair down like this in front of a woman." The ambience was cheerful and light, and we didn't do or say anything to bring our affable friends down.

The last comedian did a whole routine in multiple choice quiz-style fashion. I was sure that if my sister Lauren was there she would have found it more funny than a guy wearing a too-tight bathing suit at the beach. "What does it mean when you hear a siren on the road?" he asked the audience. Then he said, "Here are the choices: (a) there's a horrible accident ahead of you, (b) there's a wild woman on the loose, (c) someone's coming to dinner." Everyone in the place roared. He didn't really want us to answer. He was just trying to get us to think. One noisy heckler shouted out, "It means my wife escaped," and everybody roared again. Michael said, "Someone must have prompted him to say that. He's got to be a part of the show," and we all agreed.

Rob was nice enough to pick up the tab this time, and it really wasn't too big since we ordered everything light. When the bright lights came on at the bar we all decided that it was time to leave. We turned down anything extra at last call and made our way to the door. Dori sensibly asked Rob for the keys and told him that she would drive since he had been drinking. Rob had his car repaired the week before because it had been vandalized. This time they parked it safely in a parking garage across the street.

The three of us were standing by the curb watching Dori dash onto the opposite sidewalk. It was on the warmer side that night so none of us were wearing heavy coats. I was just about to turn to Michael and Rob and remark that there was good karma for Dori this evening with her choice of a dress and no real fashion mishaps when, out of the blue, a herding dog ran off his master's leash and tried to back Dori into a corner. He jumped up on her once, leaving four dirty paw prints on the suede material of her dress, but his owner grabbed him back in time before he could bite her or do any further harm. She frantically screamed this time. "I can't believe it! You're going to pay for this!" Then she just looked as if she was going to cry. We dodged across the street to make sure she was all right, and then we tried to cheer her up. "Now, there's your comedy skit," Rob said.

Dori showed her graciousness as a good sport once again and accepted the dog owner's apology. "Tina, design me an outfit not made from any animal skins or furs, please. A *Tina Fashion* that I can call my own and wear without worrying about encountering impending doom in this animal-friendly, God-forsaken cool city of ours," she said. "No problem, Dori. We're so sorry. Maybe the stain will come out," I answered. Dori replied, "This one is going in the Goodwill box. I'll never wear it again in NYC. In fact, you'll never see me wearing any part of any animal anywhere in the USA again."

I was a tad bit happy that all of those accidents had converted Dori, who had a great fashion sense, into a non-animal wearer, but I couldn't help but feel a tiny bit sad for her run of unfortunate events. Then I reminded myself that each time something bad happened, it could have been worse. The dog could have bitten her. The crane could have fallen directly on her or Rob, and the paint could have been poured directly over her head to ruin her lovely hair. She got off easy. "If you dressed down and blended in with most of the crowd on the busy streets, your life wouldn't be nearly as exciting, Dori. You're a wealth-flaunting woman in every sense of the word, and that's what's getting you into trouble. To tell you the truth, I'd be curious to see what unforeseen attention you might capture in a *Tina Fashion*. Let's try one out next time. Anyway, we've never had a dull moment out with you two on a date. *Saturday Night Live* could be having a field day with you."

Chapter 15
The Scheme

The next few days I worked diligently in my studio on vexing designs that were eccentric and somewhat provocative. Even designers have to move with the times and break tradition every now and then to keep new and refreshing styles unique for the younger generations. I sketched patterns for skin-tight Lycra pantsuits and matching wide lapelled belted jackets with big, black, round buttons, slinky nymphatic gowns in an array of colors, and feminine embroidered three-piece business suits.

My artistic talent was ongoing as I planned out the kind of simple stylish clothing the world needs today. As I finished each sketch, I clipped the paper to a board hanging high up by the high intensity lamp. I liked to look at them in a line to pick and choose which ones I liked the most. Sometimes I'd call Mary in to ask her for her opinion. The charcoal pencils and the deep pastel crayons she had ordered were new and long and were making my work easier. Right away Mary picked out the bright yellow suit. "This one is very classy, Tina." It's fit for someone in the White House," I agreed with her wholeheartedly. "Matched up with a pair of olive green leather gloves and a clutch bag, it would be perfect for a formal day affair."

Mary ran to do some errands outside the office, so I decided to call Lauren in private to see how things were going. I was dreading the conversation, but I picked up the phone anyway. It turned out that I didn't have to be the bearer of any bad news, because Lauren quickly rambled on to the troubling topic. "I am totally aware of everything wrong in my marriage, Tina," she said. "In fact, Jimmy has confessed to me about his affair, and we have already sought out a marriage counselor. We've been meeting with him twice a week on a regular basis ever since."

All right, I'm not going to need the roll-on deodorant after all, I thought. *But if I did need it after working up a sweat about my sister's situation, it would be the kind that doesn't leave powder marks under my arms on my good clothes.* I felt so relieved that I didn't have to slip her the gossip about her husband's behavior. "You see, Lauren, you still might be able to patch things up. It seems like the two of you are willing to try and save your marriage." Lauren answered, "I know. But for me especially, it's been very hard to deal with this problem emotionally, and I'm not into taking any meds right now. Popping antidepressants only seems to make me tired. I still need to do something impulsive on my end, just to let him know that I mean business."

After about an hour of talking on the phone, we came up with a simple plan to make Jimmy jealous. I decided to arrange a purely platonic meeting of a sort for Lauren with Michael's friend Chris—the one who did the lighting for the magazine covers and the one who is so generous with the compliments. "It would really be a type of blind date, disguised as a small impromptu gathering at my place. If you dress right, Chris will be naturally flattering. But if I coach him on what to say and do, he will be all over you, and Jimmy will be fuming. I know Chris will go along with the scheme. He is such a nice guy. He also has had his own experience in the troubled-marriage department, and I know that I won't have to pull his sleeve," I said.

Lauren was reluctant at first to say okay, because she felt it was a little immature to play this kind of head game. But finally she agreed to go along with it. "What the hell," she said. "It's worth a shot. I don't have too many opportunities in front of Jimmy to make him jealous. That really is part of the problem in our stormy marriage."

As soon as we ended our conversation, I called Michael and asked him to please invite Chris and his photographer buddy Joe, and Rob and Dori to a little impromptu party on Saturday night. I told him Mary, Lauren, and Jimmy would all be there for a casual evening. Next I explained to him in detail about the plot to make Jimmy jealous. He knew that a more serious scheme was warranted in their relationship, so he said, "Yes. Chris will get the point of the plan, but I won't let on to everyone else what's going on."

"I'll keep it simple, with appetizers and cocktails, and maybe we can play a game of Mind Trap. Then we can wind down with dessert and coffee before everyone leaves," I told him. Michael did not waste any time in calling me back to tell me that everyone could make it.

I worked a few more hours in the studio, flashing bright ideas for more trendy, carefree clothing. Before completing my work that day, I came up with a fantastic design for Mary to wear to one of her formal time-share dinners. She had asked me awhile ago to send my current brainstorming technique in her general direction. A ruby, red-spangled, one-shoulder minidress was what I designed for her. With her body shape and coloring, it will be perfect. When I called her in, she fell in love with it right away. "Can you give me the paper with the design on it so I can take it directly to my own personal seamstress?" she asked me. "Of course, Mary. If sewn correctly, on you it will look sensational."

The seminar and dinner combo is a significant annual affair for Mary. Some guy in the Virgin Islands had observed her keen secretarial skills right away the first year she attended. I think it was somewhere around 1999. He was impressed with her work ethics and her sense of style, and he gave her the position of apprentice immediately. I later learned that he was a very wealthy man, and he had no family to pass his money down to. I think he thought that someday Mary might move there. I always knew that he played only a father figure in her life. Maybe it was a mistake to think that. It's years down the line now, almost a decade later to be exact, and I really can't be sure of anything except that Mary will never move away from NYC. Around me, she always seems more attracted to younger men anyway. She only has a few more weeks to plan for this, and I can tell that this time she really wants to intrigue someone. She won't lend me any more information, and I won't ask. But if she wants to tell me her affairs, I'll be there to listen. For all I know there might be a young diver or scuba instructor attending the dinner who wants to take her to *Carnivale*.

"I'm going to close up shop now and go to the store to pick up some things for tomorrow night. You'll be there, won't you?" I asked. "Sure, it's been ages since we've hung out together," she replied.

Before Mary left, even though I wasn't going to, I filled her in on our somewhat immature scheme to make Jimmy jealous. "It will be interesting to watch what's going on behind the scenes. He deserves a little peek of what he exhibits," she said.

"Please don't ever let him know of our private plan. We may be dressing down a little here, but it seems that he and Lauren have a slight chance at some kind of positive future. Right now, however, she has absolutely no outlook on life."

"Don't worry, Tina. I won't make a big project out of it. I'll carry it with me to the cemetery when I die, and they can engrave the words '*Here lies a secretary with a secret*' on my headstone. Hopefully, I'll be the only one there wearing red."

Chapter 16

The Get-Together

With my fashion design mannequins hiding behind the curtain, my studio apartment was the new stage set up for Chris's new role of photographer's assistant turned actor. I was the person in the audience who couldn't wait to see how he carried off the part. The intercom buzzed loudly to begin the scene, and it was Michael who came on first. I met him in the middle of the stairway to help him carry everything up. His great-smelling men's fragrance diffused through the hallway, and he looked very handsome, as always, in his brown sweater vest and faded blue jeans. When we filled up the ice bucket and put the last bottle in the cabinet, Rob and Dori arrived carrying some good stuff. Then, as was contingent on

Michael's guest list, Lauren and Mary walked in together, followed by Chris, Joe the photographer, and, finally, Jimmy lagging behind. The men shook hands, and the women all hugged and greeted each other. They all stood in the lobby for a while as Michael served cocktails and tried to loosen everyone up. He didn't feel that it was necessary to hire a bartender to mix drinks at this small and very casual affair.

Lauren looked pretty in a mint green, tight-fitting, turtleneck bodysuit and a pair of mint-green-colored denim jeans. She appeared taller and younger than ever because she was wearing high bronze slingbacks and her hair in a different straight hot-iron style. She had a braided bronze belt around her waist, and she was carrying a matching clutch bag. As soon as Chris spotted her, he said, "Hey, sexy."

Jimmy overheard the comment and quickly interrupted his advance by saying, "You know my wife Lauren also happens to be Tina's sister. I'm her husband, and I've held that position for many years." And so the evening got off to a terrific start.

Dori kept to her newly made-up, astute, "No-animal-fur-or-skin-in-NYC" rule by wearing an ankle-length black dress with a lacy V-neck and flouncy wrist sleeves. She had a bit of trouble reaching for the appetizers, because the bottom of her sleeves kept dipping into the sauce. They were impossible to roll up, and everyone laughed when she said, "I think I'll pass on the shrimp toast."

Rob was involved in a deep conversation about public transportation in the city with Jimmy, who inadvertently admitted that he frequently uses taxicabs to get around. I met eyes with Michael after that comment and quickly looked down so he wouldn't pick up on it. Chris was moving in closer to Lauren because she was looking at a gold-framed picture hanging on the wall of the two of us taken about twenty years ago on top of the Empire State Building—now, of course, the tallest building in NYC. "You don't look a day older," he said, as he put his arm around her shoulders to get a closer look.

"Do you mind if I light up a cigarette," Joe asked, not wanting to infringe on the moment. I didn't want to say yes because I really hate the smell of second-hand smoke. So, like all of the new, stringent no-smoking laws in NYC, I followed suit with a suggestion to take it out onto the balcony. He was very agreeable, and it really didn't seem to pose a problem. In our close circle of friends, only Dori and Lauren smoked occasionally, but really only as an excuse to get out of the house. In fact, almost everyone had given it up years ago. I guess we all either grew up or became health freaks. Ignoring the surgeon general's warnings in this day and age didn't make any sense to me at all. Of course, I kept that to myself so as not to appear the ex officio on the matter of good health at my happy social gathering. And I didn't want to put a damper on Lauren's evening, which was going so nicely.

About five minutes later, when I was passing around

the appetizers, we heard a slight scream coming from outside. It appeared that Dori had intruded on Joe's cigarette break, and as he was flicking his lighter, the sleeve of her dress caught fire. Being a photographer, he was so used to bright light that he didn't notice the flame right away. Rob swiftly came to her rescue by throwing a bottle of water on her arm. The material had been dangling low enough so her wrist and hand did not get burnt, but once again her dress was ruined. "You're three for three now, Dori," Rob said. "Perhaps you should get rid of your entire wardrobe and wear your birthday suit next time." When everyone realized that she was all right, she laughed a frightened laugh. Her face wore a grimace, and this time around she wasn't that much of a good sport handling her accidental fashion abuse. "I'm just about to transform myself into a plain Jane for the rest of my life," she said.

Mary was perched on the edge of the microfiber sofa reapplying her red lipstick with a tiny, round, pocket mirror. She was busily chatting with Michael about Fashion Week and the city's plan to move the tents from Bryant Park farther up north to Lincoln Center. Michael's firm was moving back to NYC to assist in the promotion of the new center. "When the Winter Gala work is over, you'll be seeing a lot more of me. I've got some significant meetings with the mayor of the city on my agenda. It's going to bring a lot of business to the heart of NYC. And it will definitely be a boost to our economy. The stockbrokers, models, politicians, designers, business owners, and residents will all be in their faded glory," he said. Mary eagerly replied, "The center will be a much richer place to deal with the members of the fashion industry. While the tents in the park were quaint, they were not adaptable in all climates to the VIPs surrounding our profession. I think the move will make Fashion Week a more formal event."

My special group of company was getting along nicely, and the small talk filled the evening. No one was in the state of mind to play games. We munched out on dessert and talked over the aroma of coffee and freshly brewed tea. I asked Dori if she wanted something to change into, and she borrowed a pair of blue jeans and a sweater from my closet. "That's better. Now everyone watch out!" she said when she came out of the bedroom with Rob trailing behind.

As Lauren walked over to place her mug in the sink, Chris came up behind her and put his hands on her hips. "You have such a small waist," he told her. "You must wear a twenty-six-inch belt." She turned around fast, almost as if doing a pirouette, and replied, "I wish. My workout hasn't been that effective yet." Then Chris leaned in to get a better look at the gold chain that was dangling around Lauren's neck, as if looking for an explanation. "Oh, it's my initial, L," she said. "Someone gave it to me a short time ago after the terrorist attack on the World Trade Center. A lot of my good friends died that day. It stands for 'Lost' and 'Lauren.'" He nodded his head in understanding as he slipped his arm around her waist. "It's very unique. You smell so good." From a distance it looked as if he was going to kiss Lauren on the neck. "It's Women's Intuition, and I sprayed it on my neck," she said. "And something's telling me that you're attracted to me. I mean, you know, the fragrance." Jimmy caught the scene this time and bolted up to elbow Chris out of the way. "I'll just get these plates out of the way for you, Tina," he said. My woman's intuition was also telling me that the brilliant scheme was going along accordingly. Jimmy was actually jealous, and he absolutely did not know how to handle it.

"What did you say your line of work is again?" Jimmy asked him. "I happen to be in public relations with Michael, but I do some photography lighting work on the side for my friend Joe," Chris said. "You know, the one who lit Dori's dress on fire. If you ever need any PR work for your wife's modeling career, I'll be glad to give you a hand. In fact, if she'd let me do the lighting, I'd be there in a flash."

"Are you kidding me? She's not a model. She's just acting like one by wearing *Tina's Fashion Designs.*" Lauren quickly interrupted the conversation with, "Jimmy, don't always take everything so literally." But it was really Chris who was taking everything literally. She didn't want Jimmy to say anything negative about her sister, the gracious hostess who was giving her the best night out that she's had in a long time. She looked up and winked at me, and I took tremendous satisfaction in the knowledge that Jimmy was getting a piece of his own fabric. He never really liked me, but now I was certain that he was becoming irked at my profession and my sister's involvement with my contacts and the beautiful overwhelming attention that his wife was getting from our good friend Chris. On behalf of my sister, this revenge looked like gold thread.

When Jimmy excused himself to go to the bathroom, Chris actually did take Lauren in his arms and kiss her. She pushed him away, of course, and I whispered, "You two would actually make a nice couple."

"Now watch yourself, Chris, or you'll find yourself on someone's hit list by tomorrow," Lauren said. She put a soft stop on his moves, but she was really enjoying all of the attention.

When it was around two thirty in the morning, Mary reminded me that she only has two more weeks before going on her island vacation, and that meant only a short time before the Golden Globes at The Tavern on the Green. When Michael mentioned the Globes and the Green in Central Park again, Joe went nuts. "That is the exact place and the exact event where I got my start as a mainstream photographer. I caught some great pictures of celebrities entering and leaving, and the tabloids were paying me right and left. You're allowed in by invitation only, and I was invited that year. Some of the stars don't like me. Maybe because some of my past photographs have been unflattering or something. But, the lighting is always good, and they are always in focus. Some celebrities I posed, but mostly I captured candid shots of them doing what they do best, modeling. With the new digital photography, I just delete the bad ones. My old camera sucked. The delay even made it hard to catch my favorite models at the lingerie show and some tennis players in action at the U.S. Open."

Michael knew that Joe's story was wrong, because the Golden Globes have never been held in NYC before, but he just let him tell his story without saying anything. Later I whispered to him, "Joe's actually a very good photographer, but he's not great at getting a news story straight. It's a good thing he's not a reporter."

"Tina was lucky enough to get two tickets for designing the gown for one of the nominees," said Michael. "We'll be attending that function in mid-March. Even if we obtained an extra ticket, Joe, it would probably be only the television crew and technology assistants allowed in."

You could tell Joe felt a little foolish, like one of the Jets blowing the last play of a practice game against the Giants, but he answered confidently enough. "Oh, without a doubt. They have excellent security and a bunch of freelance photographers would never be allowed in. I much prefer doing cover shoots for magazines and the like. I really hate being categorized as part of the paparazzi."

Lauren was having such a good time that she did not want to leave. Of course, Jimmy forced her to call it a night. Chris managed to squeeze in one last hug before the night was over. "Maybe I'll run into you around town sometime," he said, while simultaneously spying the glaring look that was coming from Jimmy. Jimmy's facial expression was a combination of "now I have to keep an eye on my wife," combined with, "I'd better be careful that no one catches me out gallivanting in the city." It was great.

Dori and Rob stayed a little longer than everyone else to help me clean up. She changed back into her dress so that she wouldn't have to take my clothes home, even though I told her not to worry about it. She turned up the burnt sleeve as Rob said sarcastically, "Let's see if I can get her home without another royal mishap."

Michael decided to walk out with them. He was going to ask me to take one of his suits to the dry cleaners for the awards dinner, but then he remembered that he had purchased a brand new three-piece suit shortly after our lunch date in the city. "It's a solid black double-breasted suit with a thin blue vertical pinstripe on the pants and jacket. The vest is a blue satin three-buttoned one with an adjustable strap in the back. Gone are the days of those annoying cummerbunds."

"Michael, it's not like you to be so descriptive with your clothing. Are you trying to impress me or something?" I asked. "I'm just joining the recent trend, sweetheart. You're the expert, not me. But I'm not really a bad dresser, am I? Too bad you had to make it in fashion designing; you're really good at hosting parties too."

He pushed me against the back of the door and leaned in for a long passionate good-night kiss. It made me feel good inside to hear all of those things from him. After we said goodnight and I closed the door, I secretly deemed the night a great success.

Chapter 17
The Airport

Mary's vacation arrived faster than the news of a celebrity breakup on the Internet. "This sprung up on me like a stretch band coming loose from a garter belt," she said as I drove her to Kennedy Airport myself in Michael's Lexus to give her a more personal departure. "I know, Mary. I just hope your thigh-high stockings don't slip down when you're boarding the plane," I said.

Very often there can be too much commotion caused by other people when traveling by classic van or limo. When it's just a short trip to the airport, it's usually much easier to travel alone. That's why I asked Michael to borrow his SUV. Mary only had a few pieces of bright blue luggage with her, including an over-the-shoulder garment bag, which had a wide, cushioned strap so it wouldn't hurt her arm. "Do you have the *Tina Fashion Original*, Mary?" I asked. "Yes," she replied. "It was the first thing that I packed. I didn't want to fold it or lay it down, so I hung it straight in the luggage I'm carrying. I'll take it on the plane so I don't have to risk it getting lost or separated from me, even though there are no shuttle flights between here and my destination."

"When you're carrying an expensive designer gown, it's a great idea to keep it with you. Once, a guy friend of mine was going on a cruise out of New York Harbor. His evening wear was lost in transit on an airline layover from a European country. The cruise line was nice enough to lend him a free tux for formal night. But it just wasn't the same. He didn't like the way he looked. There will be no substitute for my authentic *Tina Fashion,*" I told her. Mary put her hand up to her forehead, pretending that she was wiping the sweat off of her brow. "Don't worry, Tina. My situation is different. I won't lose it. Thanks for customizing the design. I really can't wait to knock the socks off some guy."

Her bags were within weight limit, so she did not have to pay any extra charges. After all, she was headed toward a warmer climate, and most of her clothes were on the lighter side. "I might have some additional space for you to stow away in my luggage, Tina. Do you want to come with me?" she asked. "I would love to, Mary, but my whole outfit would get wrinkled," I replied. "Besides,

I've got to attend the Golden Globes, remember? I have a feeling that this is the event that's going to send my career skyrocketing!"

"I'm sure Melissa Tray will blow some luck your way. You'll have to fill me in when I get back!" she replied. "Make sure you get Michael's Lexus back in one piece!"

Mary was going to be boarding soon, so I didn't give her a long, drawn-out good-bye at the gate. "Have a great time!" I said as I gave her a quick hug. "The work will be here when you get back, so don't worry about anything while you're away!" I knew that she was not the type to worry about anything anyway. For as long as I've known her, she's given the world the "it's not a problem" attitude. I personally love her relaxed nature. That's what makes her such a great match of a secretary for me.

The precise gatekeeper scolded her for not having her boarding pass ready, so Mary told her to "chill out." She fumbled in her pocketbook until she found it and proceeded through the tunnel without looking back. She purposely lagged behind a cute band member who seemed to be in his late twenties as if she was playing a silly game of "me and my shadow." He was carrying a duffel bag and trying to brush the hair out of his eyes. *Just her type*, I thought to myself. She was starting the trip in a playful mood, and I was sure that she was going to have some exciting encounters along the way.

Before heading toward home myself, I snuck into the gift shop to purchase a pack of Orbit whitening gum and a magazine. High up in the center of the wall, a flat-screen TV showed *CNN's* breaking news that a hurricane was headed for the islands. If Mary had heard that news before getting on her plane, she probably would have told the pilot to fly into the eye of the storm. Luckily, it was supposed to be changing direction soon. I just prayed that Mary would be in the clear and that the hurricane (named after me) would blow some good luck my way at the Golden Globes.

As I proceeded through the walkway in the airport, I passed a whole crew of flight attendants, a pilot, and a copilot dressed in full uniform. I just had to marvel at the professional way they carried themselves. I took a wild guess that they worked for an extremely popular American airline and that they were headed toward Europe. The pilot and copilot were both in dress blues with gold buttons and white caps with wings on the sides. The stewardesses were wearing blue skirt suits with thin straight-line skirts, short man-tailored red jackets with wide collars, and little square pillbox hats on their heads. They were stylish in a very old-fashioned way. I thought that following the old rules of satisfying weight limits and keeping model looks as a prerequisite for airline personnel were long gone. But looking at this group of people, I could be wrong. I wondered if they still serve the meals and beverages on the flights with the same polite manners and sophistication as in the past. This group would probably even offer you a pillow upon boarding.

That's so nice when you're buckling down for takeoff. I wished that I had designed their uniforms myself. They were classy and fitting for their professions. Perhaps someday I will do just that. *Tina's Whirlwind Fashions.* Now I knew my mind was getting a little distracted. Somehow I got lost in the crowd and then decided that it was time to leave.

As I cautiously pulled out of the parking lot in Michael's Lexus, I realized I was being followed by a burly man with a white beard, a gold hoop earring, and an armful of colorful tattoos. He had a 35-millimeter camera on a cloth strap around his neck, and I surmised that he was in search of a story. He was either after me or Michael. I tried to drive really fast because I was fleeing from the man, but the traffic on the expressway was like a zipper with a piece of cloth lining stuck in it. "If only I could fly over the road in record-breaking time, like Santa Claus at the end of the parade," I said aloud to myself over the volume on the Sirius radio. Somewhere around Thirty-fourth Street the man's red sedan got stuck at a light, and I lost him. Because it was very windy, the car was shifting left and right, making it hard to stay in the lanes, but I kept both hands on the wheel and managed to maneuver all right. When I passed a major department store on the right-hand side, the bump in the road made my head hit the roof of the car. I chastised the construction workers in their reflecting green vests standing on the side of the median. "You really should have that fixed!" I shouted.

The last thing I need right now is a concussion before the Golden Globes. The workers seemed to find the situation humorous. It was almost as if they were placing bets on how many people would hit their heads while going over the hump. I was just relieved to be far from the big guy following me.

As I bolted in the door, I remembered that I had suggested to Mary to lock up the tickets to the award dinner. She had a small safe near the bottom of her desk, and I did not know where she kept the key. I wasn't frantic, but I realized that I had about a good two hours before I could contact her to find out where she hid it. Her cell phone will probably have to be charged upon arriving at her destination. If she has the key with her, she'll have to overnight it to me, and that will put so much added pressure on me and the whole situation.

I searched my walk-in closet high and low for the right hanger holding the dress that I was going to wear to the award dinner. It was a white, beaded, floor-length, skintight gown with thick ribbon straps at the shoulders and a satin sash underneath the chest that tied in the back in a big bow. I labeled it a *Tina Original*, and it is one of my most expensive designs. I planned to wear a pair of white satin pumps to match and white diamond stud earrings very close to the ear. Underneath the gown I would wear a white strapless bra with white lace panties, thigh-high stockings, and a garter belt. The gown was wrapped in clear plastic, so I left it that way and just hung it on the back of the door. Then I proceeded to lay out all of the accessories so each item could be easily reached.

Being so prepared and well organized today did not calm me down any, because my biggest concern was how in the world I was going to get the tickets out of the safe in time. This was almost as bad as burning a last-minute hole in an outfit with a hot iron. It wasn't Mary's fault, because she had enough of her own things to take care of. This was not a deliberate misdoing but a sheer matter of forgetfulness. If worse comes to worst I'll have Michael blast the safe open with a stick of dynamite or a combination of highly explosive fireworks. That's how much I am looking forward to going to the Golden Globes. I know the safe is fire resistant and shatterproof, but I do not know its capacity when subjected to the force of gunpowder. In my mind the whole matter resembles a NYC scene from an old-fashioned comic strip. I hope it doesn't come to that. After all, I'm a designer, not *Brenda Starr*.

Two and half hours later, the phone rang, and it was Mary telling me that she arrived at her time-share safely. I patiently waited for her to tell me of her travels, and then I slowly asked her if she knows where the key to the safe is. There was a long pause on the other end of the line, and then she burst out laughing. "You didn't think I brought it with me to the Virgin Islands, did you? I would have had to overnight it or something. Tina, listen carefully. The key is on a chain hanging on my bulletin board. It is the only silver key amidst a handful of gold ones. It is also slightly smaller than the others, so you should have no trouble finding it," she said.

"Jeepers creepers, Mary. That's one thing you should have told me before you left. Melissa Tray would have thought we are all a bunch of airheads," I replied. "Thanks again; I'll talk to you soon. Enjoy your trip!" As soon as I hung up the phone, I found the key, opened the safe without much of a hassle, and there before me were two gold and black Golden Globe tickets to The Tavern on the Green for tomorrow night. They almost felt fragile in my hands, and I quickly locked the safe again, this time hiding the key in the back pocket of my jeans. I figured Michael and I could make a quick stop here right before leaving for the catering hall just to be on the safe side—no pun intended.

I had planned on going to bed early so I could possibly look well-rested for tomorrow night, but there was too much interesting gossip going on here in the city—and on NYC television.

With my universal remote, I searched for important news between channels: The Yankees won again … Someone got their uniform dirty and is dating the "*Material Girl*" … The Mets fans are getting out their T-shirts for Citi Field—Good-bye Shea … Another politician is in trouble with his wife. Her scarf is lovely, though … It's going to be really windy tomorrow night, with remnants of Hurricane *Tina*, that changed direction and is now headed toward the East Coast ... *The Late Show* host is wearing a gold tie.

I shut off the TV by midnight before his first guest even came on. But, it seemed the whole rest of the world stayed awake to roam NYC in a path of multicolored lights outside of my window. Before shutting my eyes, a larger-than-life figure wearing Melissa's sapphire gown moved in ascending waves down the street. It was really only a mirage on the windowpane caused by the blue headlights of an oncoming car.

Chapter 18

The Golden Globes

The pre-fanfare escapade went as smoothly as the freshly zambonied ice at Wolman's rink. We were sitting in a glass-enclosed room looking out on scenic Central Park two and a half hours prior to the start of the award ceremony after having dressed, showered, and unlocked the tickets without another catastrophe. Michael told me that I looked sensational in my white evening gown, and, to tell you the truth, I felt very glamorous for a change. I even polished my nails in frosty pearl white for this occasion and managed to scrub the ink off of my palms. The catering hall's empty stage looked like a blank page in my sketchbook, soon to be filled with a crowd of nervous words.

We were seated at a round table for ten with a crystal chandelier hanging overhead, and there were very ornate calligraphic plastic-covered menus in front of us displaying the fare for the night. I wanted just to nibble on something light and take the edge off the hungry feeling and butterflies in my stomach. Michael, on the other hand, wanted filet mignon in *béarnaise* sauce with sautéed mushrooms. I finally decided on stuffed flounder with lemon rice pilaf. The basket of buttered rolls on the table were simply delectable, and they came with a variety of flavored butters on the side.

Many of the nominees were pouring champagne to calm their nerves, and there was a lot of clinking of glasses and chattering going on. Michael was rattling off names of stars that he spotted and tapped me on the shoulder when we were going to encounter a brush with fame. I was, of course, paying close attention to what everyone was wearing and taking my own inventory of what was working for someone and what wasn't. I didn't recognize anyone too famous at our immediate table, because most of the high-profile stars were seated closer to the front. I just figured the people seated at our table were behind the scene talents, relatives, friends, designers, wardrobe people, writers, or foreign film stars. Anyway, it was so exciting being in their presence.

I caught a glimpse of Melissa entering the room through the wide French doors in the back, and she looked incredible. My *Tina Fashion* was exquisite on her in the sapphire electric blue color that somehow brought out her brown eyes. The deep, plunging neck flattered her immensely, and she was showing it off quite nicely with a pair of dangling, triangular earrings. The horizontal lines and flouncy bottom were captured by the seamstress correctly showing off Melissa's great figure. Her appearance in real life beat last night's optical illusion. She made her way over to our table after finding her place card and said, "Tina and Michael, how are you guys?" She seemed a little more nervous than usual and didn't continue with anymore conversation right then. I could tell she just wanted to find her table and prepare for the unexpected. Michael managed to whisper a compliment to her that put her at ease. "The dress is magnificent on you, Melissa. You lit up the room when you walked in," he said. "Get the hell away from me. Do you mean it? I have to find my seat now; I'll see you both later," Melissa said.

I flipped through the program while Michael finished eating and contemplated who the director was sitting across from me. I couldn't match the picture with the face, but I know I've read his famous name numerous times when the credits rolled in so many movies I've seen in the past. The energy in the room was overwhelming.

When the lights dimmed and the drum roll began, there was a silent gasp and then thunderous applause. They started with rows of Golden Globes dancing to musical scores from the top five best pictures. It was upbeat and lively and a great way to draw the crowd into the show. The grand finale of the introduction was a made-up silly song by the presenter. "*Hollywood, New York. I want to wake up in a city that's not asleep … It's not up to you … Hollywood, New York …*"

The presenters for Melissa's category were two good-looking actors in sharp tuxedos with black velvet collars and red rosebuds on their lapels. The one who was slightly taller than the other held a long, black, gold-sealed envelope in one hand, and a shiny Golden Globe award in the other. There was a glass-enclosed podium with a curled wire microphone and a black step stool–type box for the younger actors and actresses, who would not be able to reach the microphone. "And the winner for best actress in a supporting role is …" It was no surprise to me that Melissa won, and her fast walk up to the stage drew a standing ovation from the crowd.

She blew a kiss to everyone at her table and then drew in a deep breath, held her head up, and flashed a squinted smile. I could tell that this was the one award that she most wanted, and this was the one she got. The presenters took a moment to kiss her on the cheek too, and when Melissa got a hold of herself she wowed us with her acceptance speech—which, rumor had it, was written by someone she knows on Long Island. She pretended to fumble for a paper as she joked that she had hired someone to write her a speech even though she didn't really expect to win. In her rambling Brooklyn accent, she said, "But it must have blown out of the writer's hands in a windstorm on a beach in the Florida Keys. It's now floating in the water somewhere near Hemingway's house in Key West, or being eaten by a shark, or maybe it's lying on the sand near some brush filled with mangroves and aloe plants, or being used by a teenager to light someone's barbeque in a campground next to a friend, who is now a model doing seasonal work with her husband and famous rock star boyfriend, who happens to dress as a girl. And he would be very mad if I mentioned his name in front of the millions of viewers watching this award show. In fact, my friend is on the cover of a magazine in a gift shop at the airport at this very moment, and she still managed to text me some of the words I just said.

No, really. Do you know how long I've wanted this award? I've wanted this for as long as I've been a fixed star in film. Receiving this award is fulfilling a dream that can only be compared to an author winning the Pulitzer Prize, or perhaps a great athlete winning an Olympic gold medal. If I were any of those things, I might not feel as lucky as I do tonight. Because, I've finally found a new fashion designer whose work I like."

The crowd gave a muffled laugh, and then there was a burst of applause. "My long list of thanks begins with the writer of this speech, and the producer, and director of this very suggestive movie, that I really didn't know if I wanted to be in, at first. I'd also like to thank my costars, who made filming this such a wild ride, and my four co-nominees, who I had to fight to get this. Let's just say I had my work cut out for me from the beginning. And, finally, I'd like to thank Tina, my friend and fashion designer for not making me feel like a slut in what I'm wearing for this very important night. I'd also like to thank all of the good-looking guys here who complimented me on my gown and not my ass." Again the audience laughed.

"She's so funny," I whispered to Michael. And we all stood up again to give her another round of applause. "I'm so happy for her," Michael said. "She looks absolutely stunning, and she has given your soaring career a jolt in the right direction."

The rest of the night was a mixture of long and short speeches, musical numbers, and sparkling desserts. We mingled, talked, laughed, and feasted on cheesecake, sorbet, bakery cookies, and flaming Baked Alaska. Believe it or not, a few young stars asked for my card after the show, and I was glad that I had a stack in my white satin clutched evening bag. I overheard someone in the bathroom saying that Melissa Tray's dress stood out on the gold carpet because it was a new design mixed with the glamour of old Hollywood. She said that it was going to skyrocket her career even more, and the people on the street love her ass because she's a true New Yorker.

Some other actress had a slight wardrobe malfunction on the way up to the stage, so she intelligently picked up on Melissa's joke too. She said something to the effect that she wasn't lucky enough to be wearing a *Tina Fashion* and that the people in the audience will just have to compliment her on the body part she just exposed. Everyone laughed, and I just looked at Michael with a surprised look, and he winked at me as if to say, "Way to go." Three other people at our table won awards in different categories, so there was a lot of camera action on our side of the room. Michael and I were embraced three times by people we really weren't too familiar with. We just kept smiling and clapping and playing the celebrity game, and I think we fit in rather well. On the whole, it was an absolutely fabulous night.

"I could get used to this kind of life, Michael," I said. "I know that it's hard work and a bitch to be famous most of the time, but the fanfare surrounding the glitz of an award show somehow makes it all feel worthwhile when everything goes as planned." Michael nodded in agreement. "I genuinely had a good time too. I think there should be an award for having the most beautiful date," he said. I decided to play dumb on that one, and I replied, "Then the guy to the left of Melissa would have an award, and she'd be a two-time winner, in a sense, and so would I."

"There you go again, bouncing back a compliment. Just take it and run with it next time. You look sensational tonight as well, Tina," he said with stars in his eyes that resembled fireworks. "Why thank you, sweetheart." And then he kissed me and the cameraman caught it. "We'll be in the tabloids tomorrow. You'd better get used to it," he said.

"I don't mind being in the news for something good," I replied. "But who knows how they'll turn this story around. Sensationalism in journalism is booming right now. And when the subject matter is fashion designing, somehow my name always appears in the middle of it. All I'd have to do is design a gown for the first lady, and I'd probably never hear the end of it. I should have caught up with her when she was here visiting NYC. A lot of reporters would consider that story more important than the passing of the stimulus plan. After all, it's human interest, baby. That's why mine is a whirlwind profession."

When the music stopped and the lights came back, Melissa returned to our table to thank me again, and we thanked her in return for the tickets and wonderful time. We congratulated her and said our good-byes quickly. After all, it was her time to shine, and we didn't want to intrude in her social circle. Besides, we really wanted to spend some time alone. We passed on the post parties and headed home content and full of conversation about the winners and the losers in each category.

Michael brought up the subject of the outrageous body-revealing, mesh gown that one of the other actresses was wearing. "She tries to shock the public, I think. Every year her dress gets a little more skimpy. The young presenter didn't know where to look. It was so amusing, wasn't it?"

"Yes," I answered. "It was a rather uninhibited gown

and her presenter was so flustered that he started to blush. We'll have to see what discerning remarks are in the newspaper tomorrow about that one."

When we arrived home, Michael played the winsome bachelor, and he stayed until sunrise. I was enchanted at the way our relationship was taking off, and I could tell that he was bewitched by our mutually stimulating attraction.

I carefully tucked away the two ticket stubs from the Golden Globes at The Tavern on the Green in my lingerie chest as mementos of a wonderful evening—which was a dance in the right direction for my career and personal relationship with Michael. I reviewed the night over and over again, and the restlessness I felt made it very hard to sleep at all. I was anxious and overwhelmed by a feeling that this sudden rise to fame would lead me toward completing my life's grand design. I considered taking a sleeping pill, but I knew that would just make it too hard for me to wake up in the morning. I had too many things to cross off my list in my packed fashion-designing schedule to risk feeling drowsy the next day.

Chapter 19

The Return to Business

Mary's plane glided in over the tall buildings of NYC like a mannequin doing a waltz across the floor of her studio apartment. She arrived home full of stories about the seminar and sporting a dark island tan that looked great in contrast to her sparkling white teeth. The work had piled up since she was gone, and I was slacking off in the neatness department. It turned out that the rich guy from the Virgin Islands who had first shown interest in her now had a gay counterpart next to him who shared the responsibilities of the time-share and more with his mate.

"Technically," said Mary, "it made my life much easier while I was there. I had much more time to socialize, snorkel, and suntan than I ever had in the past. There were some windsurfers on a group trip sharing one of the condos at the end of the complex, and I spent most of my time with them. They even came with me to the dinner, and I felt sensational in the ruby-red spangled minidress that you designed. It's a good thing I was wearing red too, because I funneled a Seabreeze and spilled some on the front. I love to be different, and the bare arms made the dress comfortable for me in the warm climate. Almost every other female was wearing something white, pastel, or flowered. You know, typical cruise wear. At the risk of sounding like a rich bitch, you could tell that mine was the only one custom designed. Come over and look at some of these pictures. The scenery was breathtaking—sea green water and tropical sunsets. It was a wild trip."

She shuffled some of the pictures that she had printed off her digital camera my way, and I could tell that she had a wonderful vacation. I filled her in on the Golden Globes and what had been going on in NYC since she left and how things were going with Michael. "It's nice to have you back. We've got a hell of a schedule coming up," I said.

"One more thing, I brought you back some coral and gold jewelry—a pair of crazy oval earrings. I hope you like them," Mary said. "Thanks. They're beautiful. I'll match them up with my coral lipstick the next time I go out."

Mary assumed her work mode very quickly, and she set

up the calendar for the month of April. "Tina, you're next big event is a charity fundraiser fashion show sponsored by the popular Fashion Institute of Technology. It will be held at Gracie Mansion. You'll donate a star design to be modeled by one of the students and give a small speech on the career of fashion designing."

"I know, Mary. They have a terrific internship program. Sometime in the future, I may be asked to take on an apprentice. I figured I'd make the decision in the early part of next year when things slow down again."

Then Mary added, "Anyway, I booked a table for eight—casually dressed party people. I figured that our usual very trendy click would attend together. The windsurfer dude is coming to NYC for a week in April, so I thought I'd ask him to go too. It's a simple wine and cheese occasion. We can make a sizeable donation for anybody who can't make it."

"Great! Anything else?" I asked. "Well, one thing that you're not going to be happy about. We received this letter in the mail from a NYC attorney who is suing you for stealing his client's design." The light and airy mood vanished quickly as my mouth dropped open. "What nerve!" I shouted. "The guy's a moron! I'm not going to worry about it, Mary. Everyone knows that all my designs are *Tina Originals*. When the time comes, I will find the proof I need, gather the sketches in my studio, and present them to the court. For now, just put the case of *Daisy Head Mayzie v. Tina the Fashion Designer* on the calendar."

"Now I have some important phone calls to return and a whole other stack of mail to open," Mary said. "Tina, go into the studio and sketch or start gathering what you need. You should leave yourself enough time. The guy called us 'a group of headless Barbies' on the phone. Would you mind calling Lauren back? She called a few hours ago."

I went into my private space in the corner of my studio and promptly returned my sister's call. I knew it must be something important, because she rarely calls me to interrupt my work. She sounded completely miserable on the other end of the line. "Our grand scheme only made Jimmy more attentive to me for the rest of the night," she said. "He was 'Mr. Wonderful' for a short time after the party. You know, whispering sweet nothings in my ear and being really nice. But then he changed outfits again. Right after that, he was back to his old self."

Mr. Wonderful—that was a name that I never thought Lauren would use in the same sentence with other adjectives describing her husband, I thought.

"Now he's just being a complete jerk to me, because he feels guilty about something. We've got weeks of counseling ahead of us. It's going to be hard for me to forgive him. But you can tell Chris that his role-playing was right on the mark. If we ever do split up, I'd like to go out with him sometime," Lauren said.

She couldn't see the doubtful expression I was wearing on my face, but I tried to mask it with a look of certainty anyway. "I haven't even spoken to Chris or Joe since the party. But, looking back on it, I do think you and Chris may make a cute couple in some future lifetime," I said. "I'm so sorry for your troubles, Lauren. Hang in there, okay? You're just a little weather-beaten right now."

When I mentioned the charity fundraiser, Lauren swiftly told me to count her and Jimmy out. She didn't want any added pressures right now in the socializing department. Lauren said, "You can relay my welcome back message to Mary, but please don't tell her too much about my stormy marriage."

"Don't worry," I replied." I'm very good at keeping things quiet. You know that."

A while later I returned to the studio to choose the design that the college girl would model in the fashion show. My selection was an aqua balloon-bottom short dress with a lace tank-top-style top with spaghetti straps. This look might be better on a smaller frame, but in the right size anyone can look good in it. I asked Mary to find out the height, weight, and measurements of the fashion design student from FIT. When she inquired about her figure to the person in charge, she reported to me that the model is waif thin and that the balloon-dress would probably be suitable for him.

I promptly got down to business formulating another spring collection of designs, including denim gauchos, flowered capris to the ankle, and wide ten-pocket bell-bottoms in white and tan. The variety of tops included shells with round necks, V-necks, and mock turtlenecks along with some frilly wide-sleeve blouses and nautical crop tops. I came up with a plethora of designs, but I knew I would not use them all.

I kept a wastebasket nearby, and if a sketch was coming out horrible I would deep six it like a basketball player. "She shoots; she scores!" I don't know why I was behaving like this. It was some kind of odd mood I was in—a touch of spring fever mixed with a dire need for a vacation myself. *What Not To Wear!*

"I want you to go away somewhere," I said, when I called Michael to ask him to invite Rob and Dori to the fundraiser, and then we chatted for a while. I mentioned my conversation with Lauren, but he didn't elaborate because he was tied up in PR work at the moment himself. He just said that he would extend the invitations as asked and that he had a bad case of spring fever too, and then he hung up.

Perhaps I was feeling a little tired and overworked because I'd been trying to do all the paperwork myself while Mary was away, and there's even more work now that she's returned. At the risk of sounding redundant, the award dinner celebrity limelight made the daily life of a fashion designer without her secretary seem humdrum and commonplace, especially this season. Every single person in the working world that I have spoken to for the past two weeks sounded obnoxious and downright nasty. I should be working on a tan on a roof somewhere in between filming scenes of a movie or writing lyrics to a song, not dealing with this stuff. The fact that we'll be hiring a college intern for next spring gave me reassurance. She may lessen the workload, or possibly increase it by making errors that have to be corrected. These were the types of remarkable thoughts that entered my mind in the office when I've been aggravated by too much monotonous paperwork. I am into the arts. I'm not happy unless I'm being creative. I had been lost without my secretary, and I wanted to go back to designing.

Mary diligently prepared some outgoing mail that required my signature, and we went through the stack together rather quickly. "You're as efficient as ever, Mary. That vacation did not slow you down a bit," I said. It was a little warm in the office so I turned on the air conditioner, and the fan almost blew Mary's papers to the floor. "Don't worry, Tina," she said. "They're not in any particular order."

When the day was over, we both breathed a sigh of relief, and I went home to unwind. I searched my closet high and low for something professional—yet sexy—to wear to the wine and cheese fundraiser. Finally I decided on a coral-colored linen straight-line dress with a wide, shiny green belt and matching pumps. I figured I'd wear the jewelry that Mary had given me and some matching coral lipstick. I was impressed with the fact that it was real jewelry set in fourteen-karat gold, and I joked to myself that I must be paying her nicely. It was so thoughtful of her to bring it back for me, and Mary always managed to show good taste. We've been exchanging wild earrings with each other for birthdays and all sorts of occasions since we were young, and, believe it or not, wild striped knee socks were favorite gifts as well.

For this event, I would arrive in a *Tina Entertainment-Tonight*-style. I was hoping to look somewhat attractive and appropriate in it at the same time. I needed to look mature and confident next to the beautifully dressed young college girls in the fashion show. My sister Lauren would probably have wanted to see me give the speech in a pair of fancy blue jeans. And to tell you the truth, I considered wearing them. But my position, status, and career in life won't allow for that look on me right now, and I love blue jeans more than anyone. My career is fashion designing, so I'll just keep my collection of favorite comfortable jeans for the down time in my studio and my days off.

Chapter 20
The Charity Event

Our private table for eight was up front in Gracie Mansion's massive dining hall, but since only six of us were in attendance, I felt obligated to make a sizable donation to the college on behalf of *Tina Fashions* for Lauren and Jimmy. I presented a check for a thousand dollars to the organizer after my speech and revealed that I would be happy to participate in the internship program next spring. She was delighted and asked me if I would mind posing for a picture with the mayor of NYC, the president of FIT, and the organizer of the charity event right away. The organizer herself was a well-proportioned woman wearing an old-fashioned navy blue and white sailor dress with a big wide collar and sliding belt. It had buttons all the way down the front, and I must say she showed a nice sense of style for a woman her age. The mayor was genuinely nice as always, and he left early to attend another function for the governor.

When the photography crew entered with their equipment, I recognized their faces immediately. It was none other than Joe and Chris, who are absolutely in on every major event requiring still-shot cameras and lighting that NYC has to offer. I know they caught me smiling because I simply could not stop laughing at the fact that they were there again. I invited them to our table to fill the two empty seats, and they said that they would come over later in the evening when shooting table shots. "I just have to talk to you before you leave tonight, Chris, about your excellent role-playing performance at my place," I told him. "I'll make sure to see you before I leave," he replied with a wink.

Michael, Rob, Dori, Mary, and her boyfriend were having a rip-roaring time passing crystal pitchers of sangria with fruit in them around the table. Slices of oranges and lemons were falling into burgundy-filled glasses. I could see from a distance that they were reverting back to their college days in the middle of this mainly younger crowd. Dori was wearing stark white jeans with a skintight, long-sleeved, all-white bodysuit that fit her like a glove. As always, she looked sleek and stylish, somehow standing out even among the younger girls. I looked away for a minute, and when my glance returned to the table, I could see a disaster happening in slow motion. Mary's boyfriend accidently knocked one of the pitchers of sangria off of the table right into Dori's lap. He tore up laughing and watched Dori react. She would either get up and walk across the entire mansion looking like she had just gotten her period or sneak into the closest bathroom and dig up a change of clothes. Luckily, one of the college girls came to the rescue and offered her an extra pair of jeans in a size ten to wear for the rest of the night. "I never seem to go home in the same clothes I arrived in," Dori said jokingly. Then she told the girl about her recent fashion disasters. "This was supposed to happen to one of you college girls, not to me. I should be a character on a sitcom or something," she said.

I was completely in awe of Dori's good-sport attitude. She is definitely not a sore loser in the big picture of life. Something told me that she is used to not having things go smoothly for her. Someday I will have to have a discussion with Rob about what kind of life Dori had growing up. Anyway, she is a great person for a fashion designer to have become acquainted with while advancing her career. I really like her. I am actually learning lessons about the dangers of fashion by hanging around with her, and I think someday that I may write a serious book on the subject.

We continued joking and laughing the rest of the night, and every now and then someone would pay attention to a model in the fashion show, and our table would applaud loudly. When my *Tina Fashion* came out, we all stood up and cheered. The balloon dress was eccentric compared to some of the traditional choices on the stage. One of the worst pieces of clothing in the show was a hand-sewn denim wraparound dress designed and made by one of the students. It was a little crooked, and the white stitches at the hemline were uneven and frayed. You could find fault with her as the seamstress and as the designer, and it drew loud boos from the audience. "I think they do it on purpose, Tina. One of the sororities has a gag fashion every year, and no one gets mad about it," Mary told me. "Oh, that explains it then," I replied.

When Chris came over to the table, he only had a few minutes to spare, so I filled him in on all of the recent happenings. He admitted that Lauren was exactly his type of woman, and he told me that if she's ever available he'd like to date her. "The flattery I bestowed on your sister that night was not forced. I'm actually very attracted to her," he said. Then he added, "Even though you've always been my first choice, Tina. Between the two of us, if I can't have you, your sister is the next best thing." I smiled earnestly, but looked at him doubtfully. "Be careful what you wish for, Chris," I said. "Anything is possible."

"Anything except coming between you and Michael," Chris said.

Speaking of Michael, he appeared to be caught up in conversation with everyone else at the table. In fact, I hardly got a chance to talk to him all night. It wasn't really a major function, and I was actually afraid that he might be a little bored. He had a faraway look in his eyes, like he was up to something, and I really didn't know what to make of it.

We called it an early night, and I grabbed the keys, volunteering to be the designated driver. Mary and her boyfriend were bordering on intoxicated because she snagged a guy too young for her again, and Rob and Dori's good mood had vanished. Michael was still quiet, and I was too keyed up about the speech and business talk to let loose and have a wild time. I dropped everyone off in order of location, and Michael was the last one to get out since he lived in the apartment right near me.

The two-story wooden mansion was beautiful all lit up at night, and we all agreed that the mayor has a beautiful place to live. I told everyone that nothing beats the lights of NYC after dark. The fast motion and action-packed lives of the people here is not something to be contended with.

As I pulled the car up to the brick building, we simultaneously caught a glimpse of Jimmy going into the *La Grenouille*. "Did you see him? He's been found out. I'm seriously going to have to set Lauren up with Chris. He showed her interest, and she showed him interest in return. Jimmy is a careless jerk who doesn't know what he's got with my sister as his wife."

That escapade clinched it for the both of us, and Michael didn't say another word about him. He just got out of the car and kissed me goodnight. "I'll call you tomorrow, Tina," he said. "Another job well done in the fashion department. I am buried in work since we relocated, so I can't say what time it will be."

I took another tactic with Lauren this time around by calling her as soon as I got home. I was not really in the habit of going out again after coming home from a date. She was half asleep and muttered something about Jimmy still being out somewhere. I felt obligated to fill her in on the scenario this time. "Come down to the *La Grenouille* with me for a cup of tea and dessert right now." She just dropped the phone, threw on some clothes, and met me out front. She just kept walking and didn't stop and didn't talk until she was standing over Jimmy's chair with his cabaret dancer girlfriend on his lap. John the Video Producer was across the table with another dancer who looked like her twin sister. "I'm not going to cry this time," she said in a crackling voice as she took her rings off and dropped them in his whiskey glass. "You're not going have it both ways anymore. I'm through with the lies, and I'm through with you."

Jimmy got up to follow her to the door and tried to grab her arm, but she was walking too fast, and she slipped out the door successfully. I didn't even look at him, and I just walked out too. I took Lauren to an all-night diner instead for a cup of tea, which she didn't take a sip of, to calm her down, and I gave her another pep talk. "It's no surprise, Tina," she said. "I've been preparing for the worst for a long time. Tonight's as good a time as any to begin my life without him in the picture."

I ended the night with, "Oh, by the way Lauren, if it makes any difference to you, Chris wants to date you." She didn't even answer me. Her eyes filled with tears, and she just walked away and went inside to try and get through one of the worst or best nights of her life. Another chapter of her life was coming to a close, but the future held countless possibilities. I tried to console myself about the situation. Lauren has everything going for her. A psychic once told me that whatever is meant to be for someone will be. And if it's not meant to be, it won't be. It didn't seem like it was meant to be for Lauren and Jimmy anymore—unless she finds a way to somehow even the score. There is no happy medium.

Chapter 21

The Romantic Dinner

Michael called the next day and asked me to accompany him to a romantic dinner smack in the middle of a hectic workweek. I hesitated at first but then finally agreed to a quiet meal with just the two of us. His heavy PR work was getting to him, and he needed to pause and bring himself down to earth. Besides, he said that there was something very important he needed to talk to me about.

Now that statement made me a bit nervous. He had been very indifferent to me at Gracie Mansion that night, and I can usually read him like a book. I knew he had the wood burning in his head about something, but I couldn't figure it out this time. Now the truth was going to come out at last. I never pressed him for any information, but

I told myself that I could take all of the emotional stuff the world was throwing my way lately. Somehow, I knew this was serious.

He made reservations at The *Trattoria Dopo Teatro* nearby, where the food and ambience received rave reviews in every single paper in the city. Translated, the name means something like "a place for dopey moviegoers." I always thought that dopey theatergoers were the ones who wore pajamas to Broadway plays. The food critic said, "There is a plate of fancy cheese on the table and freshly baked loaves of Italian bread to munch on while you're waiting to be served." The name of the restaurant had originally escaped my memory, but Mary said that the taste of the sauce and atmosphere resembled the old Mama Leones, which moved to the Hamptons. The old housewives used to copy her by cooking in gray housecoats and buns. The new NYC socialites who moved out to the Hamptons all seem to dress beautifully now. If you can't be a fashion-plate in the city, the beach is the next best thing. As for tonight, I was definitely looking forward to relaxing right here. My mouth was watering for some nice home-cooked Italian food.

During the day I met with a few potential clients who were interested in my designs. Mary had come up with a new idea to set aside one day a week for consultations alone. I kept my graphic design book close by and pointed out the details of my work, answering any questions they had for me. I didn't clinch any deals that day, but some huge accounts, including a major department store, were going to get back to me.

At six o'clock I went home to shower and change into something dressy. I carefully chose a black skirt and a blue colored shiny satin blouse. I was trying to get ready in a hurry. My fingernail put a snare in my stockings, and I had no choice but to run back inside the bedroom to change. If the run was high enough, I could have put a dot of clear nail polish on the end to stop it and worn them anyway. This was a no-nonsense trick Lauren and I learned in our younger days. After all, the cost of pantyhose was steep back then, and sometimes we couldn't even get out of the house without a run. The new fashion world seems to be ditching stockings for perfect legs, but a pair of lacy tights or leggings will never go out of style. Since the run was way too low, I quickly found a pair of black fishnets in one of my night table drawers and slipped them on, thus taking care of the problem.

When Michael showed up at the door holding a spring mix of flowers, I lightened up a bit. Perhaps I jumped to conclusions in trying to analyze this date because I was dwelling on the demise of Lauren and Jimmy's relationship. "Oh, thank you, Michael. They're beautiful," I said. Then I carefully proceeded to cut the bottom stem of each one of the flowers and put them in my Waterford Crystal vase with water and a teaspoon of sugar to help them grow. "This will only take a moment,

Michael. I like to put them in water right away. I have to try and keep them alive as long as possible."

We headed to the other side of town, holding back our conversation until we were seated at the table. Even though it was a weeknight, there was a nice crowd waiting to be seated. It was very dark in there, and fancy yellow candles were flickering on every table. Wine racks filled with glass bottles lined the shelves, and gaudy Italian tiles decorated the walls. There was a glass case by the front door filled with cream-filled *cannolis* and other Italian pastries. "I'm not leaving here without ordering dessert," I said. "They all look so delicious."

I was still a little confused by the inexplainable look on Michael's face as I tried to placate my own fears of soon hearing news so unfathomable that I may not be able to deal with it. When the waiter came over, I ordered chicken *parmigiana* and spaghetti with a tossed garden salad and Italian dressing. He ordered the veal baked the same way, but with a side order of french fries and house dressing for the salad.

"I am not going to baffle you any further, Tina." I felt like he was breaking up with me or canceling something on layaway. "When we went on that first lunch date in NYC, I wasn't totally honest with you about my past insignificant relationships. The truth of the matter is that I fathered a son with a woman that I have absolutely no feelings for, and she's in the city at this very moment. He's only two years old, and I had no idea that she was even pregnant. She wasn't wearing maternity clothes or anything. But when she brought the boy to my office the other day, you could see that the striking resemblance to me is amazing. Anyone looking at him would be able to tell that he is my son even without a blood test. It really freaked me out."

I sat stunned and stone silent while this news sank in. My presentiment about some kind of approaching misfortune was confirmed. It just goes to show you when you are a woman, you should never doubt your own intuition. There are always strings attached.

When you feel that something's wrong, then something's usually wrong. Finding out that my premonition was correct was indeed disturbing, but the fact that he was bringing this out in the open so soon after finding out himself made me somehow accepting of the situation. *Handling this like a grown-up is the way to go*, I told myself. I'm a career woman first and foremost right now, and nothing in my life will ever rattle me. Even if Michael and I decided to get married, I could incorporate a family life in with my fashion career, right? I just assumed it would be my child, not someone else's.

He just sat there searching my face for a reaction, and when I was ready to speak I pushed the candle on the table out of the way and leaned in really close. In a very low voice I said, "Your unusually quiet demeanor with me yesterday and the day before led me to believe that something was wrong, Michael. I know you too well not to notice changes in your behavior. But with all of my inner strength, I'm going to tell you not to worry. I won't let this little snag ruin our growing relationship. Besides, I love kids, and if your son looks anything like you, he's got to be adorable. Oh, and you seem to have spilled a little spaghetti sauce on your shirt."

Michael breathed a sigh of relief and then smiled as if he was wiping sweat off his forehead. "I wasn't sure if you'd be understanding about this, Tina. You really are too good to be true. So now's as good a time as any for an impromptu proposal. Everything's been going so wonderfully with our relationship up to this point since I've moved back. I've suddenly realized that I'm in love with you, and I don't want to lose you over anything. Will you marry me? We can go ring shopping tomorrow afternoon."

Again, I sat stunned and silent. "Of course I'll marry you. But we'll have to work together in all aspects of life—careers, children, clothes shopping. Okay?"

"Anything for you, sweetheart!" Michael said. And he ordered a bottle of Italian wine to celebrate. And this time, I drank along with him.

Chapter 22

The Engagement Ring

The next day, there was a glistening jewel present in NYC. The sun in the sky wasn't the only thing shedding light on the subject as we headed toward the old diamond district without telling anyone the news of our engagement. This was going to be too much for everyone to take in right now. I figured it would be better to hold off on the so-called press release for a while, until everything was official. Michael did take me to his office first to meet his son and the woman that he had been tangled up with. They had arranged a meeting before she was to leave for the airport. The boy's name was Michael Jr., and he had dark brown eyes and brown hair similar to Michael's. He really was as cute as a button. The mother was a big, blonde, German woman with blue eyes. She was sporting a natural, no-makeup complexion and wearing a zippered-front polyester jogging suit. She told me that the whole situation was awkward and that she couldn't wait to get the heck out of NYC.

Michael told her that they would have to correspond by e-mail about child support and visiting rights and that if she needed help in any way to give him a call. He did and said all of this information in front of me without hiding anything. After all, the kid was going to be a part of my family in the future. Business is business, and I knew this all had to be taken care of matter-of-factly with the boy's well-being in mind. I'd be helping Michael to dress him, feed him, and love him soon enough.

We went to lunch to change over the troubled-situation mood to one of genuine happiness about the unpredictable future. Somehow my appetite disappeared, and I poked at a chicken Caesar salad with my fork, barely finishing half of it. Michael wolfed down a turkey club sandwich and thanked me again for being so understanding.

"Michael, I know how things happen, and we weren't even going out at the time." He sensed that I was in a hurry to curtail the subject. "Let's just finish eating so we can go ring shopping."

He paid the check, and we walked out into the bright sunshine. Then I grabbed his arm to pull him away from a swerving taxi that was zooming past. The white and orange taxi beeped with a loud horn, and we nearly jumped out of our skin. "That was close," he said. "See, you saved my life."

"Someone doesn't want me to marry you," I replied.

After much consideration and intently looking at every single gem in the city, I decided that Michael would make the best husband. I carefully selected a huge clear-cut diamond with a unique custom-made round setting. The circle is a symbol for the never-ending life that begins with marriage. It had a very high fourteen-karat gold setting with six prongs. With the diamond in it, it looked like a thirty-carat rock or something. Anyway, it was very different than any other engagement ring I've ever seen. Michael knew a lot about diamonds because he'd been doing some research on the computer. "You have to look at color, cut, and clarity when choosing one, Tina," he told me. "And most of all, check to make sure there aren't any big flaws or chips."

We studied each diamond through a magnifying glass as the expert filled us in on what else to look for. He gave us an exact appraisal certificate for the one I chose. It cost Michael a ton of money. The jeweler whisked it in the back to begin the work of sizing the ring. When he polished it, it was like he was primping a model for the runway.

The person behind the counter told us that it would be ready in an hour. Michael couldn't believe that my ring finger was so small. I was exactly between a five and a half and a six. The salesperson suggested that I go with the bigger size. He said that I could always wear a ring-guard. But, I wanted it sized exactly to my finger without being too tight, like a form-fitting dress. I planned on wearing it all the time, and I didn't want it to fall off. It was almost the most expensive ring in the store. And to me, it was the most fashionable of all.

We sauntered down the block for a while to get an iced coffee. "Tina, I thought you were going to take me for all I'm worth," Michael said. "You could have sent me scurrying to invest in some stocks on Wall Street, you know. I have some excellent competition hanging around the Financial District." We both quickened our pace, as we made our way back to pick up the ring.

After the transaction, Michael carried the tiny black velvet ring box out and proceeded to get down on one knee in front of the jewelry exchange. He flipped the ring box open, and this drew a crowd around us. I had the feeling that this was commonplace on this side of town in diamond city. Michael didn't skirt the issue. He just made it sincere and to the point since he had already proposed once before. This was actually somewhat of a replay of our feelings. "Tina, will you marry me?" he asked while he slipped the ring on my finger. "Yes," I answered. And then I threw my arms around his neck and all of the people around us started to clap and cheer and shout, "Congratulations!" Even more people started to surround us to see what the commotion was all about.

Another couple shouted, "May this be the start of a long and happy life together!" And somebody else gave their input. "It's so refreshing to see a man and woman tying the knot!"

Honestly, it could have been a scene from a movie. I decided not to tell anyone for a week or two. I wanted the unexpected but welcome appearance of Michael's son and the happy news of our engagement to be two separate stories. The funny thing is, no one even noticed the engagement ring until I told them—not even Mary, and I was working in close proximity to her the whole time. I even had a French manicure, and they didn't even notice.

Chapter 23
The Discovery

The plot began to unfold like a man's new dress shirt with straight pins sticking out everywhere. "It was a form of entrapment," I explained to Lauren the next time I saw her. "Like when a police officer is framed into using a drug or prostitution ring. Your husband, Jimmy, was seduced by the twin sister of John the Video Producer's girlfriend. By day, she is a magazine staff writer for *Vanity Fair* magazine, with easy access to the Best and Worst-Dressed Lists, and by night she is a cabaret dancer at *La Grenouille* Cinema along with her fraternal twin sister. She was the one that slipped the Mickey in my punch that day at the celebratory brunch in the beauty and fashion director's office. I went on one date with John, that obnoxious guy, and she was so jealous that she tried to sabotage my career and ruin your marriage. And it was the lousiest date on record."

"But, Jimmy bit, Tina!" Lauren said. "He fell for her. He fell for her low-rise jeans, her belly-button ring, and the whole easy scene without thinking of the consequences. And after so many years, that shows he doesn't love me or the kids."

"No, Lauren. It shows that he was tempted and the vicious bitches played below the belt. You have to give him another chance. You have to go to counseling if he's willing to go again."

"Oh, he's willing to go, all right. The messed-up floozy he got involved with doesn't know the first thing about what to do with the kids, and he must have dropped at least twenty pounds since this thing surfaced. Jimmy absolutely hates living at his brother's house. He hangs around in a terry-cloth bathrobe all day. He has already asked me if he can come home."

After I discussed my discovery, which was loyally relayed to me by Mary in the office yesterday, I moved on to share my good news with her. Lauren was very happy for me, and she, like me, took the news of my engagement and future motherhood with a speck of glitter. "Congratulations! I wish you guys all the best!" was all she said.

Then she asked me to design an outfit for her to wear on her date with Chris. "She's not going to forgive Jimmy that easily," I said to myself. I knew that she had to try and even the score if she wanted her marriage to work. But I hoped that she wasn't going to transform herself into the slut of NYC by giving it to every guy on the face of the earth. She was just going to pretend to give the city her version of "a cheating woman," but only with those guys she felt something for. You know, the guys she felt some kind of chemistry with—or maybe just the nice dressers.

It was an extremely strange way to share the news of my engagement to Michael with my sister, but considering the current situation, it was the only appropriate way to do it. I slipped her Chris's e-mail address privately given to me at the charity fundraiser without feeling guilty about it at all, and I went home to do some more fashion work. I reminded myself that this was what was so great about my career. It was flexible and enjoyable, and I could work when I wanted to.

Mary formulated a press release for the local paper, in case the people out there wanted to know about *Tina the Fashion Designer's* impending marriage. After our pictures at the Golden Globe Awards showed up in the tabloids, we were celebrities. At least they were decent photographs. For the next few weeks I received tons of cards and letters and congratulatory notes. All of my fashion followers wanted to know what my bridesmaids would be wearing and why the Golden Globes were strangely held in NYC in March. My business associates wanted to know what date they should leave open on their calendars. Dori and Rob wanted to be given advance notice to plan a safe, comfortable dress for Dori to wear to the wedding. The magazine editors all wanted to know if and when I'd be coming to their cities. The opera singer wanted to know which songs to begin practicing. Chris and Joe wanted to be hired by us to photograph the wedding, and Michael and I started talking about eloping.

Chapter 24

The Week for Fashion

"For me, making a fashion statement in NYC is a little like being the architect of a building made out of toothpicks at the Forbes Museum," I explained to Michael. "Without being politically correct, some people understand the concept of the design, and some people don't understand it at all," I said.

"But either way, you both enjoy listening to the comments from observers," Michael added.

"Whether it is positive or negative feedback, it takes more skill and creativity to perform the task than people realize. The glue for the architect is like material to me. They hold it all together. The toothpicks to the architect are like models of my fashions to me. Without them, our work couldn't be displayed, and we wouldn't be uniquely popular."

"Unless of course, the architect stands there and holds up the structure himself," Michael said in jest. "Or you wear one of your own designs."

Everyone who was somebody was here to kick off Fashion Week that day, along with the distinguished mayor, who is a nice dresser himself and who always seems to notice a well-dressed woman. Michael had an awful lot to do with organizing this event. The politicians and their secretaries had called on his public relations firm not long after the close of the Winter Gala and shortly after the move to the new location. The Lincoln Center this week was the place to be for famous faces and plenty of fashionable ladies and gentlemen. It was promoted so well. "I guess not one person will make the mistake of showing up at the former Bryant Park," I told Michael.

"I am absolutely honored to receive the key to the city for my work in fashion and my close ties to the Fashion Institute of Technology," I said. I could tell that the mayor liked the fact that I agreed to take part in the internship program to pass my knowledge of fashion design along to a young student apprentice. "I am a firm believer in concentrating on today's youth and education, and making room in all professions for new talent," he told me.

In just a few short years, I myself had swiftly moved from my rookie position to established fashion designer with the help of actress Melissa Tray, Mary, Brenda the model from the Spring Collection, the beauty and fashion director at *Vanity Fair* magazine, and this very popular mayor of NYC. I liked the fact that he cheerfully marched in every ethnic parade. He persuaded everyone to wear kelly green on Saint Patrick's Day—even though his jacket looked more like clover. And he eagerly participates in the start of Fashion Week every year. He is a gentleman and a scholar, and now he has become close friends with my fiancé, Michael, because of his fine work in public relations. I suddenly felt very important for being recognized by the general public and impacting the fashion world.

I made a short speech thanking him for the key, complimenting him on his attire, and praising his genuine spirit of comradeship in happily partaking in all of the exciting and cultural events in NYC. "I will keep this key as a reminder of achieving recognition for fulfilling a lifelong dream in fashion designing. And for living and working in one of the most artful cities in the USA." The people of New York especially love this stuff.

There were flower-splashed sundresses, western shirts, suede boots, conservative business suits, and pants of every length floating around the city that day. Smiling, joyous people expressing their personalities with their choices of clothing; some more than others impressing the heck out of everyone on the street. I myself was wearing a tight, straight khaki skirt with a black round-neck T-shirt and big black sunglasses.

After the ceremony, the mayor invited us to a luncheon at The Lincoln Center Outdoors. Michael told me that his public relations firm relayed a message to him not to reject the mayor's invitation—not that we would anyway—and so we were treated to a splendid meal of stuffed flounder and rice pilaf with lemon wedges. It was delectable and a surprise treat to attend this outdoor affair in the daytime. It was set up so beautifully on round wrought-iron picnic tables with colored cups and umbrellas on each one. I was directly facing the sun, so I was glad that I had my sunglasses on.

One of the women at the dais had on a *Tina Fashion* that I had designed more than five years ago. It was a crocheted peach dress with a satin slip underneath and a big peach picture hat. She looked lovely in it, and I had to tell her that it was a superb selection for Fashion Week. The mayor nicknamed her "The Dame of NYC." She was classy and old-fashioned and looked as if she just stepped off of a movie set. There were Danish pastries on the tables in little round wicker baskets, and a band was playing on the roof of one of the buildings. In between sets they were dangling their microphones over the side. All of this was going on behind the police blockades. It was an elegant and festive celebration. "Now everyone in the city will dress up all week with or without the fanfare," the mayor said.

There was a small fashion parade featuring all sorts of colorful bonnets. There were store-bought hats and homemade hats with birds and feathers and all kinds of things sticking out of them. If Dori had on the hat that she was wearing the night of the crane accident, she would have fit right in.

"This seems to be the time of year when the people of New York come together," the mayor said. Then he turned to Michael and asked him if he would like to help with a Memorial Day event sponsored by the art museum. "Definitely," he replied. "The outdoor events draw the biggest crowds this time of year."

Michael was very excited when the mayor reminded him of the summer events—including the Macy's fireworks display by the Gruccis over the Hudson River, and a possible new Operation Sail in New York Harbor on the Fourth of July. "All of these should provide you with lots of public relations work for the city," he said. Now Michael's career was on an upward spiral too.

When it was time to leave, I asked a clean-cut police officer if I could walk around the barrier to use the ladies room in one of the hotel lobbies. He obligingly slid the barrier out of the way, even though it was heavy, so I wouldn't have to climb over it in a skirt. "You're a sweetheart for doing that," I whispered. "I'm having an emergency here." He just laughed and said, "Don't worry, honey. It's my pleasure."

On the way out of the ladies' room, I ran into Rob and Dori, who happened to be standing on the purple patchwork carpet in the hotel lobby. I should have known that Dori would never miss the Fashion Week kickoff. She was wearing a pink trench coat, and her belt was hanging down the back and hitting the floor. It was sophisticated and pretty and appropriate for today, but Rob must have stepped on the belt, and it was dragging.

"We really should go out and tell Michael you're here," I said. As we started to walk away, one of the housekeepers, who was vacuuming the lobby, accidently sucked up the end of Dori's belt in the vacuum cleaner. Just as it pulled around the last loop sort of like a snake, Rob grabbed it and managed to pull it back out. "I saved your belt," Rob said to Dori. "But it seems to be covered with cigarette butts and ashes. I'm sorry my reflexes weren't quicker on that one. Maybe it wouldn't have gotten so dirty. I was hoping that today would be a day without a fashion blunder."

With a filthy belt, Dori backed out of Fashion Week faster than a writer pulling an unedited version of her self-published book. She told me that they were leaving and that they were going to leave the explaining to me. Of course, Michael thought that the whole situation was funny, considering Dori's track record.

"I completely understand why Dori does not want to dance around NYC with a dirty belt at the start of Fashion Week, with all of the newspaper reporters wandering around with their camera crews. She doesn't want to be caught having a bad day when it really counts. Especially since she really is the type of person who pays attention to fashion and appropriateness on a daily basis. She tries so hard to dress nicely and is an ace at handling the fashion mishaps with a sense of humor. I'm *Tina the Fashion Designer*, and in my opinion, she's an amazing dresser," I said to Michael.

Michael told me that Dori told him that she actually did make it into the newspapers several times when the function was held at the park recently. "Perhaps that's why she displays such graceful acceptance every time someone ruins her outfit," he said. "She is and always has been everyone's competition."

"You should say that in front of her, Michael," I told him. "With her list of fashion disasters lately, she might like to hear it."

"I'll be sure to tell her the next time we go out," he said. "The sangria spilling on Dori at Gracie Mansion could have been made into an *America's Funniest Video* entry. But, if the scene was taken out of context, he could have managed to ruin her well-dressed reputation and managed to taint some more publicity for you and FIT."

"Please don't mention John's name in front of me. I hate him since that horrendous date. I really hate him for superimposing our heads on an X-rated DVD in an attempt to ruin my reputation. And since his cabaret girlfriend's twin sister slipped me a Mickey, and hooked up with my sister's husband, I have no use for any of them. What's worse, none of them are behind bars, and Dori could technically be the next one to be stalked by that madman with the video camera."

Michael punched me on the arm lightly and said, "Spyware, Tina. He hasn't been charged with murder. He's just an arrogant son of a bitch."

"But he gets away with murder, Michael. Are you sticking up for him?" I asked. He didn't even bother to answer me.

Chapter 25

The Dance Performance

The motionless mannequins in my fashion studio did not do my newest trendy designs justice because of the lack of action. As much as I imagined them dancers, there was simply not enough activity going on. So, the special dance performance at Radio City Music Hall was enchanting entertainment for me. The live entertainers that I had designed the costumes for wore bright yellow billowy dresses with high-neck sheer lace tops and matching headbands. They all agreed to choose taupe stockings and yellow ballet slippers for easy movement. They did a theatrical number to the song "Yellow," and it was a stunning demonstration of grace and talent, to say the least. The *Tina Fashion*

Costumes were flattering to their long legs, and the synchronized line kicking during the encore splashed bright color across the stage. I was named in the program as the fashion designer, being given the major credit for this show's wardrobe.

As I flipped through the booklet a second time, I grabbed Mary's arm and said, "Now we'll have to fight the competition for the '*Christmas Spectacular.*' The Rockettes usually wear those cute Santa Claus outfits, but I'm going to try and take this winter show to new heights in the future with abstract designs in primary colors."

I struck up a conversation with the old lady next to me, a tourist with a squeaky voice and salt and pepper wire-like hair. "You're going to tell me that everyone in this city pays attention to fashion, right?" she asked. I pointed to Mary, who was looking down and smiling while trying so hard to rip open a pack of Twizzlers. "We both grew up here, and we are still among the small group of true New Yorkers who want to see what everyone is going to come out wearing each year," I said to the lady, finally revealing my identity.

"I'm envisioning a deep green, velvet, one-piece jumpsuit for this upcoming Thanksgiving parade routine. That's where they always give a little hint of what's to come in the show for the holiday season. Most fashionistas who attend the annual Christmas tree lighting at Rockefeller Center buy tickets for a Broadway play as well," I told the lady. "There is an allure of fashion here during any season, and a show gives everyone an eminently good reason to dress up."

At intermission I kept thinking about the role fashion plays in current culture and society. "When you hide something in the back of your closet long enough, Mary, eventually it comes back in style," I said. "But your body changes over the years, so they may not fit you when the style returns."

"That's right. Some people hold on to certain looks because they like the style of them, even if they are outdated. Regarding fashion, there are those who usually take the traditional approach and those who take a contemporary approach. As time passes, the latest fad can become a traditional article of clothing. Blue jeans will always be in fashion, but they are not always in style. Straight legs, plain pockets, button fly, high-waisted, bell-bottoms, hip-huggers, low-rise, boot leg, flair, acid wash, indigo, patched, relaxed fit—we have them all. Don't we?" Mary asked.

"Yes. But not too many Broadway plays show the leading ladies wearing them," I answered.

Near the conclusion of the show, I pointed out to Mary the familiar name of a well-known musician in the program who happened to be in the pit. "I had actually run into him not too long ago on the subway. He was wearing a long, black, wool, button-down coat and carrying a hard black case holding his instrument. If I remember correctly, he played a shiny brass saxophone, and he was very good at it. By now he must have a long list of credits ranging from Broadway productions to television specials included on his résumé. There was a quote by him in the newspaper one time, shortly after the news articles about that famous benefactor making the munificent donation to the philharmonic orchestra. I clipped it out and showed it to Michael. It said something like: 'The news of significance in the music community can seem obscure to those people who are mostly into fashion.'"

"Some newcomers to the city have a vague grasp of what goes on here in small social circles," Mary said. "But those of us who were born here have a strong hold on the city's unflappability regarding current newsworthy events."

"I have a feeling that's why the woman Michael got mixed up with wanted to get the heck out of the city right away. She doesn't have the same poise and self-assurance as we do. Right, Mary?" I asked.

"For God's sake, Tina," Mary answered. "Michael said that the woman lives in nylon jogging suits." Then she smiled and looked at me with an understanding look and kept walking toward the door. "That could mean she has more confidence than we do."

I could not believe that Mary was taking a neutral side with regard to Michael's affairs. She wanted to rib me but instead said, "That's it, Tina. I'm just going to keep it in the closet. A comment like that against the mother of Michael's son may come back to haunt me."

"Now let me give you some advice," I told Mary. "Don't tell Michael that I didn't like her jogging suit. It will make me look petty and insecure in affairs of the heart."

"You're absolutely right, Tina. I'll keep my mouth shut from now on about what she was wearing," she answered.

We walked around the city for a while, and dashed into the candy store to get a bag of M&Ms. There was a group of teenage girls in there talking and laughing and deciding whether or not to purchase an imitation designer bag from a street vendor. The scene was bittersweet, and it brought back memories of us following the latest trends when we were that age.

Outside we could see that the tallest girl, wearing a pair of authentic suede boots, settled for a black leather shoulder bag with a silver buckle for twenty dollars. It looked just like real leather. They walked for blocks and blocks window-shopping and talking, until finally they wandered into the subway staircase for the ride home.

Rush-hour traffic was starting to build up on the streets, and a row of fire engines sounded shrill piercing horns and sirens as they made their way through lanes of cars. "I wish I had earmuffs on. The other drivers should really pull over to the right," I said. "Two seconds to let an emergency vehicle pass could mean life or death for a person in certain circumstances."

"That irritates me too. People have to go back to being more considerate," Mary added.

On the way home, we stopped off at Lauren's apartment to see how she was doing. She gave us each a Buttercup cupcake, which she had in a white bakery box on top of the microwave. She had a collection of mugs in her cabinet for every special holiday, profession, and name encompassed in her household. I was drinking my beverage out of a bright yellow ceramic happy face. "Don't you have any fashion designer mugs?" I asked her. "I'll tell you what. I'll get you one when you make your fortune," she replied. "It will say '*A Whirlwind Profession*'." She was kidding around that intelligence and looks must run in our family, because her next plan of attack for revenge against Jimmy, or at least a retaliation, showed signs of genius.

"I am going to don a wig and go undercover as a waitress at the *La Grenouille* Movie Room. The classified ads in today's newspaper say they're hiring waitresses and dancers. That way I can befriend the two twin sisters who tried to ruin my life to see what makes them go, and either catch Jimmy with them or surprise him enough to win him back," Lauren said.

"I hope it works, for your sake," was all I could come up with. "It's kind of a last resort."

"If nothing else it will be a fun trick to play on the two evil sisters. If they never find out, it will still be interesting for us. If they do find out, it will be the best trick ever played. Go for it, Lauren," Mary said. "As long as you have waitressing experience, you're in. Be sure to wear something sexy for the interview."

"Okay. Please keep this quiet from Jimmy. This is going to be the greatest risk I ever had to take."

Chapter 26

The Revenge

[Lauren looked as pretty as a Broadway actress sashaying out on stage for the first night of a performance. Her own shoulder-length highlighted blonde hair was completely hidden by a shiny, dark black, *Chicago*-style pixie wig with straight-across bangs. She applied fake midnight black eyelashes, which were curled and long, so you could barely tell it was her. The ivory dress pants and pink silk blouse that she wore just to go in and fill out the application were businesslike and sexy.

The hardest part of the plan was meeting the manager wearing a phony smile. She really didn't know what to make of him, but he sure knew what to make of her. He seemed to take a liking to her right away. She used Mary's

185

address on the paper and gave Mary's cell phone number as a contact number. "I see that you have an impressive background in waitressing," he said, as he checked her and her credentials out thoroughly.

Lauren's alias in her new persona was Paula Wilkinson. It didn't take long for her to warm up to her new name and occupation. "Paula, you can start tomorrow night at six thirty. We'll need help setting the tables and dealing with the hungry dinner crowd. If you serve them well, you should make some nice tips, sweetheart." He licked his lips and straightened his belt buckle, trying to send her a ridiculous signal in vain.

Lauren grimaced as if she was boiling inside, but she just pasted that fake smile on and said confidently, "Thank you so much. I'll see you then." The manager wasn't really a bad guy. It was just the way he had a habit of talking down to the ladies. She didn't like him for the very fact that he hired and managed the obnoxious twin sisters. She hated them for good reason. It was the whole dramatic scene she despised, with her unfaithful husband smack in the middle of it.

Before she left, the manager handed her the short, black, fringed, flapper-style uniform on a wire hanger covered in plastic wrap. She ran right home to try it on, and it fit like a tight one-piece flexee. She didn't waste any time changing back into Lauren. It was like magic, with everything, including the wig, tucked away for the dramatic scene. She couldn't wait to call me and Mary to tell us that she got the job. "Scene one of plan A, 'The Retaliation,' is officially in full swing," she said.

When I hung up the phone, Mary and I discussed the fact that we should frequent the *La Grenouille* while Lauren is working, just to keep an eye on her. "I want to make sure that she doesn't get into any trouble with the evil twins," I explained to Mary. "I have visions of them locking Lauren in the bathroom in the back and sealing the door with duct tape. Or drugging her and taking obscene photos like they did of me."

The night rolled around fast. Lauren transformed herself into Paula as easily as she did the first time she assumed the role. The costume, makeup, and wig put her into character without her even having to try.

Her shift started promptly. Lauren efficiently set up several tables with napkins, silverware, salt and pepper shakers, and a rack full of artificial sweeteners. When the dinner crowd shuffled in—mostly couples—her work became more difficult. By eight o'clock, the clientele were mainly guys, who immediately started to give her a hard time. When they tried to run her ragged, or unravel her, she swiftly put them in their place.

"I really wasn't too worried," she told us later, "because I knew that I could handle myself. But, in the first hour, one guy reached out to pinch my butt, and I turned around and snapped his elastic," she said. "His friend told him to knock it off. Most of the time I was just a good sport. I pretended to play along with the guys without actually giving it out."

Lauren kept a keen eye on the door just waiting for Jimmy to come in. The dancers arrived at nine o'clock, and the manager forced some introductions. Everyone was too busy to really get into each other. When the music began, the other two got on stage to do their thing. Paula took a coffee break right in the middle of their intermission. She headed for the ladies' room knowing full well that the two of them liked to touch up their makeup before going on. The lighting in that room was as bright as an auditorium during a play's intermission. She hid in the stall and stood motionless until, sure enough, the door opened, and the twins walked in. They were only fraternal twins—not identical—but you would really have to know them well to tell them apart by their speech and mannerisms. One had a slightly sharper nose than the other, and one weighed a tiny bit more, so it gave her face a fuller appearance. The long, straight, shiny dark hair obviously ran in the family.

"What do you think of the new waitress?" one asked the other. "She seems like a pretty, spoiled, stuck-up little bitch who's used to getting her own way," the other one said. "But we won't let her even get close to John or Jimmy, will we?" she asked. "In fact, if she knows what's good for her, she won't go near any of our favorite men," she added. "Or she'll find herself tripping with her tray over my heels."

Lauren kept her breathing still, but she couldn't help smirking. *It's my first night here, they don't even know me or my situation, and this is how they talk,* she thought. *I'd seriously better watch my back.*

"John called me to say he and Jimmy will stop by for a drink around ten o'clock," one of the twins said as she applied her orange-blaze lipstick. "We'll be extra attentive to them tonight. I overheard Jimmy saying that he's trying to reconcile with his wife, and we can't let that happen, can we?"

"It's showdown time already," Lauren said to herself. "The curtain is up, and we barely had time to get into our costumes."

Lauren looked in the mirror to make sure that her wig was on properly. She took a drop of water to smooth down any flyaways, but there really were none. She was careful to avoid the high-hat lighting and any other obstacles. There was a full-length mirror on the back of the door, and she checked the back of her stockings to make sure that the seams were straight down the back of the legs. When she was certain that everything was in order, she went back outside and grabbed a tray. "If this waitressing gig was permanent, it's no cushy job," she said out loud to herself. "Some of these glasses and plates can be very heavy."

Lauren tried not to spill anything on her flapper costume. She carefully placed a round of *Margaritas* at a table where four flashy females—wearing very ornate and colorful flowered dresses—were having a conversation in Spanish … "*Usted es vestida es bonita … Gracias … Nada de sol en las copas.*" They were trying to tell Lauren to tell the bartender not to rim the glasses with salt. She was only able to catch a little of what they were saying because she had taken French as a language in school. There were some similarities in the words, but they were talking way too fast. "*Estupido …*"

The manager came over as soon as he noticed their dresses and heard the scuffle. "Paula, take them back and wipe the salt off the glasses. We'll lose a ton of money if we pour those drinks down the drain." She just nodded and ran in the back to follow his orders. "As long as they don't see crystals anywhere on the glasses, they'll be all right with the same drinks," he said. He spoke loudly to Lauren, and she hoped that none of the Spanish women were able to translate what the manager was instructing her to do in English.

Just a few minutes later, Jimmy and John entered the club dressed in long shorts and high white socks. These two had some kind of buddy-bond going on, and they were punching each other's shoulders and acting very immature. John's eyes were glued to the stage, and Lauren posed as Paula to take their beverage order. She just looked down at the writing pad and didn't look directly at them, but she could feel Jimmy's eyes looking her up and down. "She's got the same birthmark on her neck as my wife," he told John, but John was too enthralled with the show to notice. The twins changed once during the show to white flapper costumes with the same swinging fringe. The guys both ordered White Russians (*Kahlua* mixed with vodka and half and half over ice). It has remained a very popular drink since the late seventies and early eighties when Russia was still a country, although the name doesn't have any significance to the subject of geography. When they were dating, Jimmy used to say to Lauren that he liked to get a fast buzz right away so he could relax and get in a social mood.

The drink put him in a social mood, all right. As soon as the twins came off the stage the guys whistled for the two girls to come over. The manager told Paula that it was okay for the dancers to sit down at the tables and take another break, but it was not okay for the waitresses. Jimmy's favorite twin came over to sit on his lap, so Lauren whizzed past the crowd and proceeded to splash the drink on his lap first. "Whoops," was all she could say as she hurried to the back to get out of the way. He got up from the table to use the hand dryer in the men's room to dry his pants and said, "Don't worry about it. I know you didn't mean it, babe. You were just fighting her for my attention, right?"

While he was gone, the twin on the other chair dropped one of the sweetener baskets beneath the pedestal of one of the tables. When Jimmy came back, he tripped over it and accidentally knocked the cabaret dancer to the ground. She broke the strap on her sandal, almost twisting her ankle, and hurried to the back for a change of shoes. Jimmy turned to John and made a comment regarding Paula. "The waitress would be kind of cute if she wasn't such a ditz."

"Hey, babe, give us another round to make everything all right."

When she turned to go back to the bartender, Jimmy said to John, "I swear she has the same exact wiggle as my wife." But John waved him off as if he thought Jimmy was full of it. This time Lauren returned to the table and set the drinks down without an accident, so Jimmy pulled her onto his lap instead of one of the twins. "You see, it's easy once you get the hang of it." The manager was outraged by his waitress sitting at the table, so he rescued her before it turned into a brawl. He yanked her up by the arm and told her to go and serve the other tables. He didn't make the guys leave, and Jimmy metamorphosed into an egotistical maniac after the second drink. "I swear that the waitress wears the same perfume as my wife," he said to John.

When Jimmy caused Lauren to drop a tray of French pastries on the floor while trying to serve the next table, the manager cursed and told her to "Get the hell out of my restaurant!"

"Hey, don't yell at her like that," Jimmy screamed as he ran over to yank the manager's arm. "It was my fault." Jimmy softened up as Lauren's eyes filled with tears. She was upset partly because she had been shaken up by the manager suddenly turning gruff, but mostly because of the fact that Jimmy was sticking up for her while she was disguised as Paula. The whole situation stirred emotions in her that brought back all of her feelings for Jimmy. When she raced out onto the street, Jimmy followed her and said, "Your eyes look so green when you cry." Lauren pulled the Paula wig off and gasped. "Just like your wife's eyes," she said. "And they've been green a lot lately because I've been crying every night knowing you're hanging around John the Video Producer and the twin cabaret dancers. You'll stick up for me dressed as a flapper-style waitress, but you don't give a damn about me dressed as Lauren, your wife."

"That's not true," Jimmy replied. "The only reason I'm out here is because you've been socializing so much with Tina. The whole fashion designing world and the people of NYC know you better than I do lately. If you'd knock it off and stay home once in a while and be a wife sometimes, I wouldn't be out so much. I'm doing a good job as a father and bringing home the dough, aren't I?"

Lauren didn't answer him. She just started running home with her heels clicking on the sidewalk. Jimmy knew better than to go back into the Movie Room to down another White Russian. He left *La Grenouille* Cinema to go to his brother's house, and from that moment on decided never to see the dancer again. Lauren blew her away in her *Chicago*-style wig and little fringed number. He felt an emptiness about being found out and felt very foolish for putting his whole family in jeopardy.

Inside, John and the dancers were openly displaying their ignorance some more. They were having a conversation about calling the paparazzi in time to release some good stuff. John had taken some great clips with his little camera. They were relishing in the prime moments, which they knew would stir up more trouble for *Tina the Fashion Designer* and her family. "You know how I knew Paula was really Jimmy's wife? She had the same 'L' initial charm around her neck that she had on when I superimposed her head and neck into my dirty video. If they were all a little smarter, they could have saved that *Filthy Floozy Fashion Designer* from further negative publicity," John said. "The initial could stand for "Lustful," one of the dancers said. "Or Luscious," chimed the other. "Or Loser," John added, in reference to Jimmy. And they all laughed a vicious laugh.]

Chapter 27
The Beauty Contest

"I'm so glad that this contestant asked me to design everything she'll be wearing in this pageant," I said to Michael as we took our seats next to Mary and the judges in the hall at the United Nations. The feeling of peaceful diplomacy flowed through the air like a silk scarf trailing a matching gown. "It seems like only yesterday that a shoe was actually thrown at the president during a press conference outside of this country," Mary said. "He really wasn't a bad dresser or a bad president. There wasn't much else he could do but duck."

I absorbed the positive feeling surrounding me as I gave Michael the contestant's fashion rundown. "She'll be wearing the patriotic costume first, representing the good old USA. It is a sparkling floor-length gown with the pattern of the American flag in the true colors of our great country—red, white, and blue, accessorized by a sash across her chest. She'll be adorned with a diamond tiara on her head in the shape of the Statue of Liberty's crown. Next, she'll be wearing a tasteful one-piece *Tina Original* swimsuit for the bathing suit competition. I thought a solid suit would be too outdated, so we are going with a turquoise, green and yellow tie-dye design in spandex material with a high, round neck just to be different. She would get lost in a sea of sweetheart necks with high-cut legs. After that, she'll wear a version of the tiered dress from the 'Spring into Fashion Collection' to answer the question in the glass booth. You know, the same one that landed me on the Best-Dressed List that time. It looks beautiful and smart on her. Finally, the contestant will be wearing a *Tina Original* black halter gown that ties around the neck for the evening-gown competition. It flows behind her with a small train so she'll look elegant while making the turn on the runway. I'm so excited; I can't wait to see who wins."

A surge of spirited sensation filled the hall as we waited for the start of the contest. Mary told a story about the time she ran into Miss Philippines at Macy's when she was nine years old. "That was way before they started wearing custom-made fashion designs. She was searching for an evening gown for the Miss Universe pageant, and I was trying on party dresses," Mary said. "As a matter of fact, seven years before that my grandmother was buying me a birthday dress when an announcement came over the loudspeaker in the store that President Kennedy had been shot in Dallas. There is never a dull moment when shopping for clothes here in NYC," Mary added. "That's why I use Tina as a custom fashion designer now. I'm a little afraid to go shopping. With TVs outside the dressing rooms, bad news travels so fast."

Michael told everyone that he had a lot to do with arranging this contest. He said that the mayor praised him on the superb public relations work he was able to accomplish in such a short time. "I had to deal with all of the diplomats who are members of the United Nations. It was extremely important to get this event right, because so many representatives from other countries are here in attendance," Michael said.

Mary shushed us when the action started on the stage. One of the females was being led out of the soundproof booth. The gowns worn by the ones left behind looked like colorful smeared ink behind the glass. They could have passed for a school of tropical fish through a pair of wet goggles. "If you had the chance to have lunch with the leader of your country, in your case, the president of the United States, what would you ask him and why?" the announcer asked. "I would ask him if he liked what the first lady wore to his inauguration," she joked. And the audience laughed. "No, seriously, I would ask him if he foresees a change in the health-care system in the near future, so that all Americans can obtain reasonable and affordable health care while raising their families and heading for the retirement years. It is a major problem in this country because of the high co-pays and increasing number of medical providers."

"Great answer," Michael said. "I told her that she would exude intelligence in that dress," I said, as they all applauded loudly. But she didn't stop there. "I would also ask him why he made the Democratic candidate secretary of state when she would have been so valuable domestically in this country. She was the one who was going to fix the health-care system and make all of the appropriate changes for the good of our country." They had to pull her off the stage. She was elaborating too much, and she wouldn't stop coming up with more ideas and topics to talk to the president about. When the music cut her short, the announcer made a joke about never before having to stop a beauty contestant short in answering one of their questions.

Michael said, "That will either cost her the crown, or the judges will give it to her outright for exuding intelligence, being excessively talkative, and for looking good in your original *Tina Fashion* while answering the question."

It was difficult for the announcer to draw more than a few words out of most of the other contestants. I honestly felt like getting out my sketchbook and writing comic strip bubbles of dialogue for them. They were either too nervous to expand or just into standing there and looking pretty. Even though they all had good figures and were beautiful in their own way, only a few of the others exhibited intelligence and personality. "USA will definitely win Ms. Congeniality," Mary said. "She's a fast thinker with a good head on her shoulders. She comes across nice, even though I've heard the other contestants view her as a bitch. Rumor has it that she already holds the title of Ms. Obscene Photogenic. I hope that doesn't pose a problem later."

Ms. France, the representative from the other fashion capital of the world, was wearing a deplorable bright orange gown. It didn't flatter her in the least, and she still made it into the fourth runner-up position. When it was down to two females, Ms. Ireland, looking lovely in a kelly green dress by her own custom designer, and our own Ms. USA, the announcer chose none other than the wearer of my *Tina Design*. I was ecstatic!

"Good for her!" I shouted. Michael said, "I guess her long-drawn-out answer to the question didn't harm her chance of winning. The judges did not find her lacking in social experience—as perhaps the ones from past pageants would have." "It used to be in vogue to act straight-laced for the judges. But, today, being a rule breaker was definitely the way to go," Mary added.

One member of the panel was a former Ms. USA. She was in the very same pageant that Mary's friend, Ms. Philippines, was in. Out of the blue, she told me that she loved my fashion sense. I was so happy to have my work noticed by someone who has the reputation of being a pure fashion plate. No one will ever be able to come up with any dirt on her. "Let's see what the reigning Ms.USA does for your career, Tina," Michael said.

When the applause stopped and the photographers cleared out of the hall, I was able to continue our conversation. "You see, Michael. This is exactly why I like doing what I do," I replied. "Fashion designing touches so many people here in NYC. A lot of people worry about what to wear on a daily basis. But, it is the hype caused by the media that causes people to think about my behind-the-camera career. When people read about fashion designing in the news and see the photographs, they seem to pay attention to who created the fashions that the celebrities are wearing. Readers like to play the 'Who Looks Better in the Designer Gown' game. Finding chic and unique clothing on the shelves and off the rack is easy enough if you know how to dress. But now a lot of people want designer clothes that are customized specifically for them, especially the very wealthy and beautiful stars in the public eye."

Chapter 28
The Apprentice

If you blink even once in NYC, a new age can blow in like an unpredicted storm finding you with your eyes closed to the latest fad. "Just between us, Mary, the internship program has opened my eyes to the irony of today's girls showing an interest in my profession. Most of the young fashion design students are more into modeling themselves at this stage of the game. Observing them at work can really be funny. They like the totally outrageous outfits on the runway that very few people would ever buy or wear—shiny leather pocketbooks worn on the model's heads, and tutu-style skirts with wire hoops—more suited for a circus than a formal affair," I explained.

Mary nodded in agreement. She couldn't wait for

the apprentice to take a break so she would be out of hearing range to delve further into our discussion. She was absolutely in hysterics after reviewing the apprentice's sketches under the bright lights in the studio.

"The girls are very familiar with the history of fashion from the animal skins of the cave women to the hoop skirts of the early 1800s, right up to today—just as we were, I think. I remember that we could not get over the fact that the females of the past wore layered clothing like petticoats and corsets just to go out and churn butter. Now, the students seem to believe that less material is more. In the case of current fashion designing, they think using wires and props add to the fashion. I keep waiting for the apprentice to draw TV antennas or to incorporate a set of tools in her design," I said jokingly.

"The front-page headline in the news the day after the fashion show would say, '*Model Snaps at Fashion Show Killing Spectator Under Catwalk!*'" Mary said.

I shook my head with laughter, took a good look at her work, and got up to lock the door to make sure that she wouldn't overhear what we were saying. "In the matter of apprenticeship, the students are eager to learn the trade or career. But they want what they want on paper, and they do not heed practical advice. The only thing is that they are correct in having the knowledge that anything goes on the runway. We have to let them be themselves. Today's fashion show producers seem to want to feature bizarre designs. The new magazines on the newsstands are proof of that. I mean it, Mary. when you turn the pages of some magazines, 'extravagant' is the new vocabulary word in the English language."

The apprentice's designs were not always worthy of praise, in my opinion. However, I gave it to her on her unusual approach. When she returned to the studio, I explained our practical art in this way. "In the fashion business, sometimes you have to be concerned with making a profit. You should pay attention to how much money can be made by only targeting the rare fashion mongers looking for unusual appeal."

Something gave me the idea that she simply was not going into this career to make money. I was the exact opposite at her age. Here we were, two people on different ends of the spectrum working together and cultivating our interest in the same whirlwind profession, and absolutely amusing Mary to the point that she had to hide her laughter a few times. The scene was a little like Barbie's fashion designer versus a Bratz doll fashion designer. It was clear to see that this choice of a career for her was not a childhood dream but instead an impulsive selection of a career. What do I like to do and what am I interested in now? She was a pick-a-major-as-soon-as-possible candidate.

But, seriously, the apprentice was a lovely girl, who was a little on the wild side. She would observe, focus, and nod her head in understanding at a custom design or sketch that I was working on, and then she'd take another piece of paper and create something totally her own. It was an admirable quality, in a way, for her to want to be original, though. If I shaded in a sketch with a charcoal pencil, she would choose to shade in her sketch with sanguine. If I designed a floor-length gown, she'd go with a mini. I liked her for the very fact that she was not afraid to be herself, and, if you can pardon my French, she was already showing signs of being a rich bitch.

I decided on the best way to teach her about the fundamentals of fashion designing. If what is in vogue during a time period displays elegance and sophistication, it is considered somewhat of a timeless beauty or classic. But, if it's an outfit that is the latest rage, fad, or craze, it's usually in and out like a flash before the world can take it in. Some lucky designers come up with a mode or style of fashion that never disappears. It's the difference between a wide acceptance of a fashion design and an adopted enthusiasm by certain wealthy people in society to have the latest style that can make or break your career.

I turned off the lamp with a serious swiftness and turned to the apprentice and said, "You have the potential to be a high-profile fashion designer in this new perfection. I began my fashion-designing career at just the right time, by first catering to the traditional. Believe it or not, you're catching it at just the right time too, by leaning toward the bizarre. Every ten years things change. And somehow or other, every fashion comes back into style. Let's just say it's like history repeating itself. The writers know it; the musicians know it; the teachers know it; the actors know it; and the fashion designers know it. I just never thought that I'd be bringing it out into the open. I always thought I'd keep it my little secret."

The apprentice turned to me and said, "So, basically what you're saying to me is that an interest in high fashion can cost you your life."

"Exactly. When you succeed in high fashion, by sheer luck or talent, the world doesn't want you to have success. And when you have it at a very young age, the world will do anything to stop you. There have been many people in this profession a lot more years than you have been. Do you understand what I'm saying? So take it and run with it. But watch your back, and most of all keep moving."

She was a smart girl. She began stacking her designs, and she never sat down again.

Chapter 29

The Wedding

The fray in Lauren's relationship was on the mend. After a tough, full year of marriage counseling, Lauren and Jimmy had finally reconciled. When the winter approached and Jimmy moved back in with her, Michael and I decided that it was just as good a time as any to proceed with our wedding. My self-designed bridal gown—with white satin hood, imitation fur, and matching satin gauntlets—were once featured in the bridal salon's seasonal show and were now hanging in a nylon zippered bag waiting to be worn. To me, the gown spoke the words "simple elegance," and, as I have said before, that is the look I am going for when I say my vows to Michael.

Lauren told me something so profound a few weeks

ago that it made me want to send out the engraved invitations right after. She whispered to me on the side, "Jimmy and I had love once. I know we were in love when we got married, and I had a nice bridal gown too. Now, for the sake of the children, we've decided to stay together to see if we can find it again." It was a positive and thought-provoking sentiment, and after seeing what the hell she'd just been through, I had the urge to shop for a trousseau and jump right in myself.

It was a wintery day, and the snow was falling in big snowflakes onto the sidewalks of NYC. Each one was like a swatch of white lace that was trimmed from a cloud in a blue fabric sky. And each one seemed to land directly on top of my head. I pulled the satin hood up over me to keep my hair dry and straight. The fashion world loved that in the newspapers the next day. Joe caught the perfect photograph of me pulling up my hood and running up to the magnificent wooden doors and stained-glass windows of St. Patrick's Cathedral. There was a bagpiper in the background standing by the limo trying to keep his plaid skirt from blowing up and exposing his hairy legs.

When Michael met me at the altar, there was a glow across his face that was actually a reflection of light coming from the votive candles along the exquisite walls. He was wearing the same tuxedo featured in the window of the bridal salon on our first lunch date here in NYC. I recognized it immediately and whispered to him that he's not an avarice bridegroom and told him that he looks extremely handsome, since he's paying for the wedding. He just shook his head and laughed, remembering what we had both said in front of the shop's window that day.

The ceremony proceeded in front of the altar before grand statues of holy figures, gold crosses, and the ornamental tabernacle until the priest said, "If there is anyone here that objects to the wedding, speak now or forever hold your peace." And for the first time in my life, I was surprised at something. Chris stood up and shouted, "Tina, you can't marry him! I wanted to be the one to wear the tux that was displayed on the mannequin in the window of the bridal salon. I've always been in love with that slim fit design, and I've always been in love with you!" He had obviously been window-shopping and drinking shots of Irish whiskey before the wedding. He had to have been to let his emotions get the best of him like that. To tell you the truth, I was so touched that he would do something so sweet, and was so impressed with his good taste in clothes, that I ran off the altar, threw my arms around him, straightened his tie, and kissed him. Then I said to him loudly enough so that everyone could hear, "Chris, I love the tux too, man. But I already made a promise to Michael, and he's already wearing it." Then, after a slight hesitation I added, "But if anything ever happens between us, or if the pants no longer fit, I will consider marrying you in a flash, on the rebound, or before it's in the news, because I will have already learned my lesson the first time around. Okay?" Seemingly pleased with my answer, Chris smiled and sat back down in the aisle seat. He turned to the guy in the seat to his right and said, "It's just something I had to do." The guy nodded his head in complete understanding. "Just pick one out of this JC Penney catalog next time."

When the crowd settled down, the priest adjusted his vestment and went on with the ceremony. Joe had a junior news-seeking photographer with him. He was running around with a pen behind his ear recording people's conversations and assisting with the lighting. I don't know if it was a good thing he was there or not. But Chris was obviously just into having a good time. I was afraid that tomorrow's headlines would read, "*Photographer's Assistant Makes Everyone Look Bad at Fashion Designer's Wedding*" or "*Bad Light Shed on Guests at Wedding Party.*"

Lauren reminded me that it is was so out of character for Chris to behave like this and that a wedding is truly a time to celebrate. Deep down inside, my woman's intuition was telling me that it really wasn't about the tux. Chris really had been in love with me all of this time, and I was blindly overlooking it. He always seemed to be in the same place that I was at the same time. He was always noticing what I was wearing. I thought maybe it was because he was Joe's assistant. Joe was the original officially intrusive photographer. He could have been just trying to impress Lauren, or trying to get her to fight for him.

The rest of the bridal party carried off their *Tina*

Original blue velvet dresses quite elegantly. Sometime between the ceremony and the cocktail hour, but after the outdoor pictures by the big tree with the heart-shaped hieroglyphics carved in it, Dori's dress brushed up against the door of the limousine. A tiny spot of grease splashed up on her. Rob screamed at the driver, "Didn't you pimp the limo before the wedding? That's what they're paying you for, man!" Michael ran over to brush the snow off of his shoulder and tried to smooth out the situation. Luckily, someone had a stain remover stick in her evening bag, and amazingly enough, the dark spot came out.

Dori and Rob are usually so cool about her fashion disasters. We all tried to find the humor in the situation because we wanted to avoid a major fight between Rob and the unconcerned limo driver. It was still snowing, and the wind was blowing a sprinkling of white dust on my hood and the bridesmaid's blue veils. I didn't know how everyone was going to come out in these pictures. We were all shivering and shaking like the steel stanchions on the George Washington Bridge. Joe picked the wrong time to try to be a perfectionist. It was against his nature. He wouldn't let anyone get back in the car until he was sure that we all had frostbite and no one was smiling anymore.

It was a wonderful reception at The New Yorker Hotel with Bavarian chandeliers and bas-relief walls. They featured a delicious dessert bar with everything from ice cream sundaes to candy apples. There was Irish coffee with whipped cream in sugar-rimmed glasses and strong dark espresso in small chocolate liquor cups. The rest of the evening was enchanting. The band's music was lively, and there was always at least one couple on the dance floor for every song. When it was Michael's turn to feed me the cake, he was very careful not to get it on my wedding gown. Dori caught the bouquet and almost fell into the cake. Rob fought off all of the other bachelors for the blue frilly garter, and the two of them turned extremely happy for the rest of the night. I didn't doubt that they would be the next ones to get married.

The entire time we were away on the honeymoon, we picked up newspapers to read about "*A NYC Fashion Designer's Fabulous Wedding.*" We kept in contact with the studio, and the public relations office, so we wouldn't miss anything that was happening. Mary kept us posted on the reviews that we had missed. We had ducked out of the wedding early to avoid additional news-hungry photographers, and we stayed in the limo a long time so no one but Joe would be able to capture a poor photograph. One critic said the wedding was very low key considering that the bride was a fashion designer. "Simple elegance," I reminded myself. "That's the look I was going for with my gown and the wedding party's attire, and that's the look I think I achieved."

Chapter 30
The Recognition

The ghosts of past and present fashion were sweeping through NYC in flowing gowns, as if they were famous actors giving their roles in *A Christmas Carol* a unique twist. Throughout history, it has been a well-known fact in society that if you are ever honored by your peers with a dinner, it is a sign that you've made it in the world. So it was a wonderful feeling for me, after clearing my slate of magazine scandals, obscene videos, and fashion disasters, to finally be acknowledged for my grand work in the fashion design industry. I was to be the guest of honor at a dinner of recognition at the New York Public Library.

It was not going to be an extravagant affair, but a lavish dinner with a few jokes thrown in, by some close business associates, patrons, models, friends, politicians, and family members. They were all saying that I had taken the fashion world to new heights by displaying creativity, good character, professionalism, and talent—while simultaneously incorporating work ethics and focusing a sharp eye on sharing an interest in today's youth so that this significant profession could be maintained through future generations. That's what they were all saying. "They" being my formidable associates in the fashion world. Now everyone knew that this was not an easy thing for me to accomplish, considering the obstacles that I had encountered along the way.

The banquet was held at Astor Hall, which had provided a lovely background for many of the fashion events featuring my designs. I had already received the key to NYC from the mayor, so this was to be considered more of a political—but fun—event. It was agreed upon beforehand that every female attendee would show up wearing one of my fashion designs. It was really Michael's idea to throw this opulent affair, whose goal is to stress the important role fashion plays in current culture and NYC society—while at the same time honoring me. The excellent public relations work and advertising drew a significant crowd of spectators outside along with a television crew. The people of NYC came up with cute nicknames for me such as "*The Diva Designer*" and "*The Clothing Countess.*" Someone even called me "*The Patriotic Pillar of Fashion.*"

Everyone entered the Trustees Room through the white marble entranceway, and I marveled at the seventeenth century tapestries on the walls. It was a great place for a fashion designer to be honored. Whoever wanted to speak went up to the podium to compliment me on my prevailing sense of style. Dori said that she finally avoided a fashion mishap on the way up to the stage. "*Tina Designs* are so versatile, they keep you from being accident-prone." My circle of friends knew exactly what she was talking about. In fact, the whole world had heard about Dori's fashion disasters.

Michael took the microphone to announce that we were officially "happily" married. He said that if he wasn't already a good dresser, he would be now with a wife who's a famous fashion designer.

Chris and Joe, the photographers, took picture after picture capturing some of my best work together in one room. They also took candid shots of everyone socializing at the dinner. They were literally flashing people, dancing, twirling, chatting, and modeling in my *Tina Originals*.

The beauty and fashion director of *Vanity Fair* magazine refrained from telling any jokes regarding the Best- or Worst-Dressed Lists, considering the recent scandal at *La Grenouille* Cinema involving John the Video Producer. They had tried to keep things quiet, but eventually it all came out in the magazine anyway because the cabaret dancer who worked there was brought up on prostitution charges and fired from the staff. The editor even felt bad about the negative publicity that surfaced from the magazine's internal matters and said that because of the circumstances, Tina has become a household name at the Condé Nast Publications office. "Tina, this dinner of recognition will probably be a feature article next month. Somehow, your name is mentioned for wearing, designing, or encountering something newsworthy in almost every issue. It just goes to show you, you're a today woman."

Mary read excerpts from the journal reflecting on my dream of becoming a fashion designer. She stood there in her custom-designed, gray, off-the-shoulder dress and affectionately read the words describing what I thought my life would be like in my chosen profession if I ever achieved success. At this moment, I realized that I had turned my wishful thinking into reality.

Finally, it was my turn to speak. When the meaning of what I had done finally hit me, I was overcome with emotion for a minute or two. I looked toward Michael for support, and he blew me a kiss that sparked my emotions like colorful fireworks over an outline of buildings. Somehow, I managed to deliver my speech with calm serenity and with what I hoped was a sense of class.

"My whirlwind profession in fashion designing has escorted me on an upward spiraling staircase to success. The knowledge that comes with this career that ultimately touches so many people at different times in their lives is really sweet. Sketching a vexing design and watching it come to life on a mannequin challenges my creativity on a daily basis. But seeing a real person wearing one of my fashions for a celebration in their life is the rewarding part for me. Everyone likes to feel like a fashionista sometimes, and when an event is of special importance, a custom-designed *Tina Original* often makes the person wearing it feel happy, beautiful, and confident. Sharing special occasions with people wearing my designs is the part of the job that I like the most. When you remember what someone was wearing for an occasion, it's like freezing a moment in time with photography. Sometimes it can be like remembering the words of a song that was playing in the background when something important happened in your life. When you choose an eccentric and provocative design from my line to show your individual sense of style for a personal affair, it makes it that much more special for me. It's a good feeling to know that someone was noticed for wearing one of my *Tina Fashions*. It should not come as a surprise to you that sharing the good times and hearing those rave reviews are what gives meaning to my whirlwind profession. I thank you all for being a part of my perfect design for a life."

I had become an accomplished fashion designer even though my reputation had taken a turn for the worst. My fundamental fashions had moved into a sexy realm, but somehow I was keeping my spotless domain as *Tina, Queen of NYC Fashion.* The rookie fashionistas and pro designers all still found my work unique.

There were a few more exciting encounters, and dangerous liaisons with the mob and crooked politicians. But, everyone looked good out there as so-called "partners in crime." Mary still funnells as my secretary, because she's still a "rich bitch." Lauren's marriage is still stormy, because of her interest in high fashion and Jimmy's roving eye. And Dori's fashion disasters remained unavoidable because she's an exciting wealth-flaunting woman. But the video producer and his cabaret-dancer girlfriends have finally run out of ways to sabotage my career, and the *Vanity Fair* magazine scandal is now considered a thing of the past. The news-seeking photographers can no longer damage my reputation with their sensationalism. I have fame and fortune in NYC and now no one can rip it out from underneath me.

This cultural period that I nicknamed the "age of fashion" continued on in NYC for at least half of a decade more. Writers were dressing up in designer clothes and fashion designers were writing. As for me, I was busy dressing up my writing, wearing T-shirts with writing on them, and designing a book. The first unedited edition of my book was pulled out of circulation (by me) for pulls in punctuation. Michael said that he couldn't even believe it went out looking like that. The completely edited version of my book finally landed on the *New York Times* Best-Dressed List. But the *crème de la crème* was having one of my most exquisite *Tina Fashions* become a *New York Times* bestseller!

Epilogue

I was always into fashion. I mean for as long as I can remember. I would sit at my school desk during a boring lecture sketching outfits and coordinating accessories. Using a pencil, I would carefully outline the clothes on the front of my folder, or on a piece of loose-leaf paper, and then I would take various colored pens and shade them in. There were blue sequinned tops with matching headbands, red silk gowns with rhinestone-edged scarves, and black and white bold flower-print sundresses with T-strap sandals tied all the way up to the ankle. My classmates thought that I was just doodling for fun, but I always had career in mind.

I knew someday I'd be sitting front and center before a runway of NYC models sporting designs with my label:

Tina Fashions. There really has been a creative evolution of fashion circulating in my brain my whole life. Once, when I went on a field trip to the Smithsonian in Washington DC, everyone else raced past the display of the first ladies' gowns worn for the president's inaugural ball. I stood there staring at the mannequins and dreaming of what kind of a gown I would design for an occasion of such importance.

Even back then, I was sure that someday I'd be in the all-important position of having to design a gown or a fancy pantsuit for the first female president in the White House. In any event, it would be something elegant and classy but distinguished at the same time. The American people would gasp at my work, and the politician making the grand entrance would come off looking polished and confident.

I think it will be a good idea to keep the name *Tina Fashions* on the labels for my designs. In a way, it will be a reflection of me and my upbringing because it's the name of a Catholic saint who did the coolest things during her lifetime. It also happens to be a shortened version of my Irish grandmother's name, *Christina.*

I envision girls all over the country asking me to design a dress for their televised super sweet-sixteen parties. The members of the band will simply fall in love with the teenagers driving up in their shiny waxed vehicles—not because of the cars, but because the girls look so glamorous. A lime green strapless gown with velvet flowers and matching patterned leather sandals will absolutely be the hit of the show. And I'll get to attend every party, of course.

"We'd like to thank Tina for her original design for the guest of honor," the announcer will say. And I will just smile and wave from the VIP section where I will be sitting and getting waited on hand and foot by a handsome bartender in a suit jacket and blue jeans.

A wedding party for an American princess will be spectacular! The bride will wear a *Tina* taffeta gown and a tooled veil with little flowered appliqués embroidered on it. White pearls will be sewn on the top, and it will be cinched at the waist. When it is time for the bride to dance, she will have her maid of honor bustle the train for her with three tiny buttons so she can dance freely without tripping over it. The entire wedding party will wear T-length pink dresses so you can see the lacy stockings and satin shoes dyed to match. That is, everyone except the little twin flower girls, who will be wearing *Tina* short, puckered, party dresses, which are more appropriate for their age group. I would never want two six-year-olds to be dressed too sexy. The entire family will be delighted with the results, and thousands of spectators will show up to watch the wedding and observe every detail as if they were all of royal descent.

My own line of clothing in a favorite local department store will be the next inevitable step. Every Sunday morning millions of Americans will thumb though the flyers taking note of what works and what doesn't. They could all be out walking around Central Park or a duck pond, but instead they will be tied to their chairs reviewing a casual line with a rock 'n' roll flair focusing on jeans and T-shirts with totally funky sayings like *"Passion for fashion!"* and *"Wearing the dream!"* They're really always so much fun to think up—a steaming tea break in the life of a fashion designer. Everyone needs a break once in a while, and everyone needs to share a good laugh. I'll just share my sense of humor with the whole world while being serious about my career in fashion.

Every time someone around you shows some personality, you can tell them that you're going to buy them a *Tina* designer T-shirt that says whatever. Suppose you work with someone who has a very aggressive nature and who is always yelling at people on the phone. Everyone is always complaining to you about how nasty he or she is. You know, the type that never gets any work done and who's always slacking off. You can jump at the chance to give them a T-shirt for their last day at the office. It will say something like, *"Make designs, not war !"* Maybe they won't get fired from their next job, or maybe they will, but at least they'll have a nice souvenir from you to look at and wear that I designed, until it dawns on them that there's a message in there somewhere.

When members of a group are at a loss for an idea of what to get someone, they will pick up a *Tina Fashion* catalog, and there will be something stylish and unique to fit that person.

No one will have to curse in dressing rooms anymore over a sash that doesn't tie, a midriff that doesn't lay right, pleats that won't fold, cuffs that don't roll. The finest materials will be used so that things won't look like shriveled up doll clothes after one washing.

My biggest challenge will possibly be designing the athlete's clothes for the opening and closing ceremonies of the Olympics—if they are ever held in NYC. Watching them will be extra special four years from now because all of the athletes will be entering the stadium wearing *Tina Fashions*. In the winter, even the ones carrying the flag will be wearing white wool coats trimmed in fur with giant hoods and crinkly white boots.

It will remind me personally of deviating from the plaid school uniforms in Catholic school on every first Friday of the month. Every other day we were as disciplined as all hell in the same skirts and white, cotton, man-tailored shirts with *Peter Pan* collars. We had it down to the navy blue snap on our crisscross ties, and, of course, the ribbed-wool knee socks. But on the first Friday of every month, we were the absolute best at showing our personalities with go-go boots, black velvet chokers, gold braided belts, and any other accessories we could find to drive the teachers wild.

Anyway, the athletes won't be able to march if they lose even one big white button, and everybody's hoods will be aligned just right so an aerial view above the stadium will show crisp winter white perfection. And I will get all of the credit. The athletes will all want to match to show their support for most of the sporting events being a team effort. And the rest of them, who perform individually, will just want to pat themselves on the back and uphold the reputation for good all-American fashion—like I do!

My line will carry through to the summer Olympics as well. The closing ceremonies for the USA teams will radiate red, white, and blue patriotism in modest, shimmery warm-up suits with drawstring pants and zippered jackets that stay open to reveal smooth Lycra unisex tank tops. They will be formfitting so the athletes' toned bodies will still be revealed. If they aren't, the members of the swim team, beach volleyball team, and track team might not agree to wear them. They are the ones who are total exhibitionists with their bodies. *Tina the Fashion Designer* agrees that they have absolutely earned the right to show off their muscles. My fashion equation for them is: medals equal muscles, plus good-looking sportswear minus calories. The Olympic fashion designing will not be the easiest work for me, but pretty much everything looks good on an athletic form. Perhaps I will be chosen to carry the torch someday.

A terrycloth headband sporting my label will keep the hair out of my eyes while I run to the top of the stadium steps and light the blaze that will begin yet another spectacular series of events. If I'm lucky, the sports commentators will notice what I'm wearing, and I'll be the next one to go down in history. Then they'll research my hometown with a documentary. When they ask my sister Lauren and my friend Mary if they ever thought that I would be the one to design the fashions for the Olympics, they will both agree that all they ever saw me doing was carrying a torch and designing fashions. They may even uncover some of the original designs created by me in the front of a purple Trapper folder somewhere in the place where I grew up. Now there's your fairytale!

I will be the one to kick off Fashion Week with a capital "F" in New York City. I may have to break a bottle of champagne across the hood ornament of a white Escalade limo or simply rip the pink ribbon from across the doorway leading to the catwalk. But whatever way they choose for the week to begin, every citizen in NYC and on Long Island will begin dressing up and showing their fashion sense. And all of the musicians and rappers will start writing songs with lyrics describing what everyone is wearing. And, of course, my name will be the most-mentioned in those songs because "*Tina's Fashions* Inspire!" All of the fashion magazines will feature my clothes, and the celebrities will wear my line for their cover shoots. The post-Fashion Week parties will keep me from my work for a while, but no other group could possibly be as much fun to party with. To have my name mentioned in those circles will be an honor and a privilege, and just being there will be the whipped cream on the *Machiatta*.

The photographers and reporters will always be checking with me for the correct spelling and description of my designs. And I will gladly give them every detail. "My label is *Tina Fashions;* that's ' *T*I*N*A*F*A*S*H*I*O*N*S* '" I will yell to them, and then I'll laugh, shake my head, and adjust my cranberry and gold buckled pocketbook over my shoulder just like a real woman of wealth. And after the party, after checking my messages on the answering machine, I'll turn on the news to see how well everybody carried it off. The Fox Five and Channel Two news teams will give me the best coverage on high-definition TV. But at least a dozen satellite networks will do some nice PR work for me. "It's human interest, baby," I will say before I decide to turn over the microphone to them—"to focus on fashion and what people are wearing, that is." And everybody will nod their heads in agreement. And for many months after, the world will be in a great mood, and nobody will get bored with seeing each other. All sorts of couples will begin hooking up again, and late-night talk show hosts may slip my name in a joke or two, so I'll be able to laugh and go to sleep peacefully for at least an eight-hour night of beauty rest before concentrating on fashion again the next day.

That's the kind of busy life and schedule I'm going to have to keep. But it's simply not going to be a problem, because I'm a superwoman in America, and this is the age of the millennium. I won't even worry too much about keeping a calendar for myself because my personal secretary will be following me with a notepad and pen, or the new generation electronic, telling me where I should show up next. And it will most likely be Mary, my good friend, who is also into fashion and doing secretarial work, or some good-looking guy who wants to be my taskmaster in the fashion business.

Sometimes I'll pull some *Tina Fashion* clothing out of my closet, and he'll press them for me with a cool-setting iron and gentle steam, so I can go to work with confidence. But if they still look wrinkled, I'll throw them back at him, in a nice way, of course, and tell him to go fetch me a true, white cotton, no-wrinkle and very feminine, pearl button-down blouse, and a new pair of *Tina* designer blue jeans. That is, only if I want to be comfortable that day.

On those kinds of days, I will want to stay out of the limelight or behind the camera and race through the stores to see what my old neighborhood is wearing for Fashion Week. I will walk at a rapid pace, going in and out of those little boutiques, with whom I have a good friendship, but I'll end up in the major department stores that also feature my name,

Then I'll buy some candy and sign a few autographs on T-shirts, flip-flops, baseball caps, tiny zippered leather-bound journals, and anything else people will hand me to sign. I will even autograph someone's cast if they have a broken leg. I'll write *Tina the Fashion Designer* in script, and they can sell it on *eBay* further on down the road.

That is, if I'm still famous then, in, say, about ten years into the future. And I know I will be famous. Because even if I'm not in the rich world of fashion then, the poor people from the Goodwill will be looking smashing sporting all of the old *Tina Fashions* that the people of the world dropped into the clothing boxes awhile back. I know that they will never really go out of style, and no matter what time of day, year, or in what country, someone will be wearing something that I designed, and they'll be feeling pretty good about themselves.

I will not be able to escape my work, and I won't want to. The computer geeks and graphic artists will have a field day making advertising tags for all of my clothing and accessories. There will be commercial ads, magazine spreads, and business cards—to name a few areas where I will need their expertise. I personally will carry around a business card in my wallet with *Tina Fashions* engraved in blue or black letters. It will have a simple faceless mannequin on it, wearing a sapphire taffeta gown, just like I used to sketch on my school folder. No face, no hair, just a figure displaying an interest in fashion that is meaningful to me and obviously the rest of the world. And each and every day, I'll wonder if I'm going to wake up soon and realize that I'm really just "*wearing the dream.*"

The End

About the Author

Catherine Miller graduated from C. W. Post, Long Island University with a bachelor of arts degree in journalism and communications. She lives on Long Island with her husband and three children. One of the many reasons that she loves Long Island is that it is in close proximity to the excitement of New York City. Broadway plays, art museums, concert venues, fashion shows, libraries, selective bookstores, historic culture, and sensational restaurants are just a short train ride away on the Long Island Railroad.

Her daughter, Erin—formerly an art student—illustrated the mannequin for the front cover of this book.

The Fashion Designer's Glossary

GALA—A gay celebration

APPLIQUES—A decoration fastened to a larger piece of material

EMBROIDERED—Designed with needlework

CINCHED—A tight pull

AGGRESSIVE—Boldly self-confident

CLICHÉ—A common expression almost worn out by overuse

SOUVENIR—Something that acts as a reminder of something

SHRIVELED—To wither or become smaller

CRINKLY—Wrinkled

DEVIATE—To stray from the norm

ALIGNED—In straight, proper positioning

UNISEX—Relating to male and female

RADIATE—To shine brightly

EXHIBITIONISTS—Exposing oneself to attract attention

COMMENTATORS—One who discusses or comments on the news

PRIVILEGE—An earned or granted right

MILLENIUM—Celebration of 1,000 years

LIMELIGHT—In the middle of attention

EXPERTISE—One who has knowledge of a certain subject

SEQUINNED—Decorated with small ornaments resembling coins

SHIMMERY—To shine with light or sheen

MANNEQUIN—A form representing a human figure

TOOLE—Material resembling netting

BUSTLE—To button in back to lift train off the floor

PUCKERED—Folded and wrinkled

CATWALK—A narrow walkway for modeling

RAPPORT—Relationship

APPALLING—To inspire surprise or horror

HUES—Orders of color

FLORID—Tinted with red

ASHEN—Very pale or lacking color

INSCRUTABLE—Mysterious

PRETENTIOUS—Too showy

COALITION—An alliance

TRANSGRESS—To go beyond the limits

CLIENT—Customer or patron

UNIQUE—Rare or special

DOWDY—Old-fashioned

FRUMPY—Drab or unattractive

SQUINTED—To look at with eyes partly closed

GESTURES—Hand signals

POISE—To carry oneself with confidence

ARROGANCE—To behave in an overbearing manner

FLAIR—A natural appropriateness

INCONSEQUENTIAL—Unimportant

DISCONCERTING—Confusing

PILAGE—-To ruin

PRATE—To babble

PSEUDO—Fake

NOMINAL—Small

GRANDIOSE—Impressive

GAUNTLETS—Gloves that extend above the wrists

STILETTOS—Shoes with pointy heels like blades

REVITALIZED—To give new life to

MERITORIOUS—Deserving of praise

RENDEZVOUS—A meeting

ENNUI—A feeling of dissatisfaction

WHIRLWIND—An upward spiral

OSTENTATIOUS—Showy

INDULGENT—To be pampered

ECSTATIC—Happy

CHIFFON—A sheer fabric

MICKEY—A drug slipped into a drink

RAMPANT—All over the place

DOLDRUMS—Boredom

INAUSPICIOUS—Unlucky

COSMIC—Vast

PROLIFIC—Productive

CONSTERNATION—Alarm

APPEASE—To calm

CHARITABLE—Merciful or kind

COMPLEXION—The appearance of the skin

SURREPTITIOUS—Secret

VICARIOUS—Imagined

NOVICE—Beginner

IRRESOLUTE—Uncertain how to be

AVARICE—Desire for wealth

ADULATION—Excessive admiring

MELLOW—Pleasingly mild

VULGAR—Offensive

DISSENSION—Disagreement in opinion

PAISLEY—A print with colorful, curved figures

LAMÉ—Clothing fabric made of tinsel-like fibers

INSIGNIA—Label or emblem

IMPECCABLE—Flawless

PROMOTE—To help advance

RETRIEVE—To bring back

INAPPROPRIATE—unsuitable or too sexy

PERILS—Dangers

FLUTED—Hollow cylinder with grooves

PEPLUM—A short section attached to the waistline

CONNOISSEUR—Expert

IN SYNC—Together

OPAQUE—Solid, not letting in light

JADED—Tired

EXTRAVAGANZA—A spectacular event

FRINGE—Straight or woven threads hanging from
the edge

CALAMITOUS—Disastrous

RETALIATION—Revenge

FAUX PAS—A mistake

BRASSIERE—An undergarment to cover the breasts

LIASON—A dangerous meeting

LINGERIE—Feminine or sexy clothes to wear to bed

PASTELS—Various light colors like sky blue or pink

RENEGED—Go back on

PROCLIVITY—Natural tendency

VITRIOLIC—Sarcastic

COSMOPOLITAN—International and citylike sophistication

FLAUNT—To show off

OBSCENE—Dirty or inappropriate

GABARDINE—A durable fabric

PLUNGING—Low

REPLICA—Copy

SUCCINCT—Concise

DISPERSING—Giving out

FOISTED—To pass off

THERMAL—Warm or hot

FLAPPER—A sexy woman from the 1920s

DEPLORABLE—Horrible

APPAREL—Clothes

SHODDY—Showing poor workmanship

HECKLERS—People shouting comments

FAUX FUR—Fake fur

ECCENTRIC—Strange

PROVOCATIVE—Stimulating

PLATONIC—Friendly

SCHEME—Plan

EX OFFICIO—Holding a certain position

CUMMERBUNDS—Colorful garments worn around the waist under a tuxedo jacket

LAPELS—Wide collars

PODIUM—Box to stand behind with microphone

REVEALING—Showing some skin

BLOSSOMING—Opening like flowers

WINSOME—Cheerful

WAIF—Thin person

GAUCHOS—Wide culottes above the knee

CAPRIS—Ankle length pants

ZAMBONIED—Ice cleaned by a machine

PLETHORA—A variety

REDUNDANT—Wordy

MEDIOCRE—Just okay

PLACATE—To pacify

UNFATHOMABLE—Unthinkable

PRESENTIMENT—Former thoughts

PREMONITION—Bad feeling

PROXIMITY—Close to

ENTRAPMENT—To lure into an act

SABOTAGE—To intentionally ruin

COMRADERIE—Friendship

UNFLAPPABILITY—Never to get rattled

PERSONA—Assuming another individual's social façade

ALIAS—To use another name

ENTHRALLED—Delighted

GRUFF—Nasty

SPANDEX—Tight stretchy material

EXUDE—To emit

CONGENIALITY—Friendship

GAUCHE—Awkward

CRINOLINE—A full, stiff underskirt

RECOGNITION—To be acknowledged for something

VERSATILE—Capable of being used in many ways

NYMPHATIC—Nymph like

FRAY—Worn to shreds

Bibliography

[Excerpts From] *Tina's Fashion Journal: What I Will Do as a Fashion Designer (NYC, 1972–1980)*

    1. Fashion Designer, Tina. *Dressing With Style For Stylish Writers (NYC)*

    2. Fashion Designer, Tina. *Stylish Writing for Models with Money (Bloomington and NYC)*

    3. Fashion Designer, Tina. *The Manual of Style for Fashion Designers : After the Recession (NYC)*

____. Second ed., *Tina's Fashion Journal* (New York: Fashion Institute of Technology, 1983).

____. Third ed., *Fashionable Essays. New York:* Fashion Designer, Tina, trans. *iUniverse*, Bloomington, IN, 2002).

____. Fourth ed., *Tina's Fashion Journal . New York: A-List: "Best-Dressed Writing" [A Novel Approach to the Role Fashion Plays in Current NYC Society] Vanity Fair* magazine, *2007.*

____. *What I Will Do as a Fashion Designer; Tina's Fashion Journal, New York, 2009.*

____. *2009.* An *E-Zine* Form Feature Publication (Dressed for the World Wide Web) ftp://ibiblio. org/personalaccount.txt. "n.p."